Just Across the River

Montana critics and historians love this book.

Toby, Julie, and Eddy are back with another action-packed adventure in Eastern Montana and beyond. This carefully crafted and researched historical tale brings the Northern Pacific Railroad story to life and is sure to keep you on the edge of your seat. *"Just Across the River"* is a first-class ticket to frontier Montana!
Rachel Phillips, Research Coordinator, Gallatin History Museum, Bozeman, Montana, author of *Legendary Locals of Bozeman.*

The author brings his Montana roots to life in this well-researched sequel to *"As the Twig is Bent."* High stakes adventure continues as Toby and Julie track a villain against the backdrop of the high-flowing Yellowstone River and the prairies of Montana.
Judy Killen, Curator, Huntley Project Museum, Huntley Montana.

"As The Twig is Bent" is an entrancing debut story about the endurance and fortitude of a youth left to survive on his own in the homestead age of central Montana; a tale of adventure for the young and old alike. The sequel, "Just Across the River", will satisfy the thirst for more about the heart-warming characters Toby and Julie. Both books are exciting, clean, and wholesome novels that shine a welcome spotlight on Musselshell Country.
Lura Pitman, Editor, Roundup Record-Tribune & Winnett Times

Dorwin Schreuder's knowledge of the area allowed him to weave the story realistically throughout Montana Territory. I certainly look forward to Schreuder's future books.

Kathleen A. Schreiber, Library Director, Harlowton Public Library, Harlowton, Montana.

Just Across the River

A Historical Novel

In Frontier Montana

Dorwin Schreuder

This is a work of fiction. Names, characters, incidents and dialogues are derived from the author's imagination and are not to be construed as real. All references to legendary persons are attributed fictitiously, and were created only to associate the work with a historical time, with no intent to aggrandize, degrade or modify the actual record of their existence. Historical and geographic references are approximate and are not intended to be exact, however most dates and references coincide with genuine archival accounts. All references to former railroad companies and associated activities, are fictitious whether or not they are mentioned in their proper historical time. Any other resemblance to actual persons, living or dead is entirely coincidental.

First Edition IBSN: 9781735580630

To my grandchildren,

my greatest fans.

Preface

This story is a continuation of the fictious lives and history published in the novel, *As the Twig is Bent,* The Tale of a Young Man in Frontier Montana. However, it would be unfair to the reader to have invested in this book and only be exposed to part of the story. *Just Across the River* is a complete saga that stands on its own. To fulfill the responsibility of providing an entire adventure, brief excerpts from the first novel are woven into the narrative here to provide a historical background for the story's continuation; but in a manner that does not spoil the plot and nature of the original. For full details of how the present characters evolved, the reader is encouraged to also read *As The Twig is Bent.*

Dorwin Schreuder

Author

Prologue

Seventy-four years ago, (1947), as a very young boy, I went with my father to gather a load of firewood. Our transportation was a 1934 International sugar beet truck. Dad's friends accompanied us in two other similar trucks. The annual search for dry pine took us just across the river from our log house resting in the valley near the south bank of the Yellowstone River. To get across the water and above the cliffs into the, at that time wilderness, we had to travel east to the Pompey's Pillar bridge, now called the Bundy Bridge. Firewood gathering was a full day's work for the adults. Only the dead dry pines, were taken from public land. There were no chain saws, only muscle powered cross cut saws. Full length logs and branches were stacked onto the old trucks, and brought home to be cut to size by a tractor powered "buzz saw."

I was immensely impressed by the vastness and isolation of the area, so close to home, but separated from me by the formidable Yellowstone River. It was my first good look at the world to the north of home. After that time my adolescence was spent on the south side, looking across at the cliffs, caves, and pine shadowed boulders to the north, longing to explore them, though they endured untouchable. I was nearly twenty when I finally crossed the barrier near our home in an old row boat. I scratched a mark in the mysterious cave that still towers above the river near my father's former farm. The journey was an emotional accomplishment, long postponed by the river.

The land between the Musselshell and the Yellowstone is now sparsely populated, but not conquered. The magic of wind scarps, boulders and seas of grass still give refuge to the ghosts of frontiersmen and settlers who lived and died there. Whenever I view those lonesome bluffs and mesas it is always with awe that I imagine the struggles within their history. *Just Across the River* welcomes you to ride into that history, and embrace frontier reality.

ONE

The west is not dead my friend.
But writers hold the seed
And what they sow will live and grow again,
To those who read.
Charlie Russell

Bright sunshine beamed through the window of Tobias Hawthorn's St. Paul office. He stared at the numbers on a calendar hanging slanted above his desk. His eyes focused on the big red number thirty. All numbers were in black except Sundays. It was Sunday, May 30, 1886. Toby loved work, and long hours, but Sunday was the special day usually set aside for his only real love, Julie. At this time on Sundays they would traditionally be together in church prior to having lunch at one of their favorite neighborhood eateries, often a hotel, inn, or stage stop. She too was an employee of the Northern Pacific Railroad, and living in the city of St. Paul. The burden of his work, as well as the company demands on her, would delay their meeting until afternoon. Both felt this was a day to be outdoors enjoying the final days of spring. But the joys of fresh air and sunshine would have to wait. Toby, in an act of desperation, and a fair amount of luck, became a railroad employee in 1881 at the age of fourteen. He was orphaned after disease eliminated his mother, and watched as a horse/wagon accident killed his father the same year. The accident occurred in the wilderness between the Musselshell and Yellowstone Rivers in Montana Territory. Toby was forced to survive the winter alone until spring, and found his way to employment with the Northern Pacific in Coulson, which later became Billings, Montana. His longtime friend Julie also became separated from her parents and was discovered by Toby, working at a Northern Pacific Railway boarding house in Miles City, Montana Territory. Through promotion and good fortune, they both now labored in St. Paul, Minnesota, the headquarters of the Northern Pacific Railway.

Toby had a brilliant mind, the result of home schooling by his mother in the remote Musselshell Country. As a child he memorized most of a Webster's dictionary, and studied writing based on Biblical scriptures. His prowess in writing and practical mathematics catapulted him into management at such an early age that Railroad supervisors found it necessary to falsely add a year on to his age to conform with employment regulations. He performed with notoriety and perfection, but his lack of socialization left him naïve and vulnerable, a trait that early in his career exposed his young age and inexperience. He was a quick learner and outgrew his social disability but at the age of twenty, he still bore the stigma of being the youngest on the staff. As a result he became preferred chattel to upper management and was consistently given unusual and difficult assignments, those with which management did not want to "muddy" their desk or reputable career. Such was Toby's predicament now.

He recently returned from a train trip to Livingston, Montana Territory, near the western edge of the railroad management division in which he worked. The purpose of the trip was to analyze the cattle shipping, handling, and procedures, because the company was experiencing losses due to missing cattle. The number of cattle arriving for market in the East, was less than the number shipped from the West.

In the short time Toby had worked for the Northern Pacific, the railroad had fallen into financial trouble. It was a very long rail route with little business. It was struggling, just out of bankruptcy. The company President, Mr. Henry Villard resigned in January 1884 due to a "nervous breakdown", and the company went into bankruptcy. The next president, Robert Harris was running the struggling business. There was a constant effort to streamline operations and revive company finances. Losses were not tolerated. Salary raises were out of the question. Toby felt he was lucky to retain his job.

Involvement with the shipment of cattle, beef, hogs and sheep was extensive during the last two years. The railroad's entire method of operation had changed to comply with new regulations. After the completion of the transcontinental connection, cattle shipments had become a major source of revenue for the railroad. Cattle were being brought from

Colorado up the Bozeman trail to Montana and loaded for transportation to the East. Ranchers all over the west were turning to the railroad to transport their cattle, rather than participate in long cattle drives to eastern markets. The Chicago Union Stockyard opened in 1865 but by 1881 it was receiving 30,000 beef cattle and 1,000 hogs every week. New laws had been passed to assure that water and feed troughs were installed into every rail cattle car, and demanded every cattle car be unloaded every 36 hours for a five-hour rest. The rest period required that rest stations be established and attended. Every small town that shipped freight had a depot and a depot agent. Many depots had cattle pens for shipping or rest areas. Cattle cars rode directly behind the engine to provide a better ride, and to make it easier to swap out the cars for the rest period. Handlers that travelled with their cattle could ride in the caboose, or sometimes called a "Drovers car", but the process was changing. Cattle producers, farmers and ranchers, had neither the time nor the will to make long train trips with their animals unless they were being transported as show animals to an exposition. The middle men were taking over. Livestock commission merchants traveled between the farms and ranches and trade centers of the Midwest. They arranged the purchase, and personally monitored the transportation and delivery of the livestock across the nation. Live animals, unlike grain, coal or other freight, still required human oversight and required personal contact between buyers, sellers and the cattle. Thus many of the middleman were also passenger train customers.

Toby had been placed in charge of cattle shipping compliance. Appointed as his assistant, was Eddy Kingston. Eddy was the first person Toby befriended when he arrived in Coulson, Montana Territory, after struggling through the winter across the Musselshell Basin. Eddy subsequently brought Toby through difficult times and as a trusted friend, Toby managed to position him in charge of cattle stops from Bozeman through the Dakotas. However, Eddy was less stringent concerning regulations, and more practical when it came to getting things done. Toby needed to meet with Eddy in person to examine possible reasons for the cattle count discrepancies. Eddy was stationed in Miles City, Montana Territory, the largest cattle shipping point on the route.

An additional problem handed to Toby by his superior, Mr. Hanson, was a collection of complaints concerning gambling in the club cars as they travelled across the Northwest. According to the complaints, professional gamblers were "fleecing" honest stockmen and other travelers during their journeys.

Toby stood up, pushing back his heavy oak chair across the bare plank floor of his office. His former boyish frame had transformed into a six-foot two-inch muscle toned superior male specimen. His thick sandy hair bent in moderate waves from his forehead to shortly above his collar. His prominent jaw often revealed his level of concentration by the firm clamping of his facial muscles. His eyes were soft blue coupled with a perpetual friendly smile. Toby was a cross between calm serenity and frightening strength. Writing instruments looked out of place in his broad muscular hands.

The light falling through his window fell brightly on his typewritten orders. The open transom above the office door was intended to circulate air into the small room. It now breathed in the beckoning smell of spring, while on this Sunday, the old steam radiator had not been adjusted for the temperature change. Its intermittent clanking was all that disturbed the silence of the headquarters' offices. He paced in a triangular path from the desk to the window, to the door, and returned. He didn't need to reread the directions of his next assignment. It was clear what was expected of him. It had been discussed in meetings for the past two weeks.

The young man was frustrated. He enjoyed his work at the time he was in Montana Territory. But he soon learned that he was capable of much more than his clerical position demanded. His superiors also recognized his potential, and brought him into the headquarters as an assistant to upper management. He knew that because of his young age of twenty years, he was seldom accepted as a serious contributor to railroad policy. He now felt he was being used as an errand boy to stamp out or cover up embarrassing problems, always making his bosses look good, while he assumed the risk of resolving problems in the nearly lawless frontier. He faithfully kept his frustration within himself. "Be of good cheer" was his motto while his attitude displayed only support and respect for his superiors and coworkers. Toby was well liked in St. Paul, but he did not feel at home. His only confidant was his lifelong friend, Julie, and she too endured similar frustrations.

He sat back into his chair and wrote a very short note to himself; a note which he would use to formulate a plan for the next few days. A trip to the western cattle shipping stations was essential. He would ride his company's train, the Northern Pacific Passenger Service to his division's western edge and beyond to Spokane. It was there that the accounting for cattle began and where most records were maintained. On his return, he would quietly investigate stock loading, rest stops, feeding stations and accounting procedures at each shipping point. After making inquiries he would discuss his findings with Eddy Kingston in Miles City. While traveling in the club car, he would observe what was being described as a "gambling problem." The trip should take a week to ten days. He hoped he would have solutions and recommendations on his return.

TWO

Across Railroad Avenue, in an annex to Northern Pacific Railroad Headquarters, Julie Carlson was reviewing her purchase orders for the next month. She too decided to work this Sunday morning because Toby was unable to accompany her to church. Her job, although for the same company, was far different than Toby's. She had worked her way up the company roster from working in, and then managing the railroad boarding house in Miles City, Montana Territory to assistant manager of passenger services. She was responsible for passenger comforts that included bedding, linen, laundry, table ware, and protocol for dining car services. She was recently given the extra duty of purchasing and maintaining an inventory of cookware for the kitchens and bar ware for the club cars.

Her office was far different from Toby's. It was 1886, a time when women were not yet allowed to vote, and work places were not integrated between men and women. Julie worked in a small space where she supervised three other women, all dedicated to clerical work. Newly invented typewriters constantly clicked in the background.

Julie was feared as much as she was respected. Feared because of her quick wit, unabashed attitude and ability to simplify problems to the detriment of her male superiors. Her physical appearance also was intimidating. She was perhaps the most beautiful female in all of St. Paul. Julie was taller than most women, but sported a frame second to none. She stood a slim, perfectly proportioned five feet nine, with wavy blond hair and azure blue eyes. Her full lips created a smile capable of warming the sourest of personalities. Her grace was beautiful in a way that made men act stupidly in her presence; behavior exacerbated by her indifference to them. She was totally loyal to Toby, her lifelong friend.

Julie was reasonably happy in St. Paul. Toby was usually nearby, and after her father's death in the Musselshell Basin several years ago, her mother had been living with Aunt Rosie only a few blocks away. However, her mother passed away almost a year ago during the summer and Julie moved in with her aunt who was now in bad health and needed assistance. Aunt Rosie was succumbing to chronic pneumonia at age 92 and was not expected to live much longer. Julie had accepted the plight of her aunt who had lived a good life and was doing the best she could to make her comfortable. Toby lived in a boarding house five blocks from the office and also helped care for Aunt Rosie when he had time.

But outfitting Pullman cars for the railroad was not her dream job. Like Toby, she longed for the open spaces of Montana Territory, Musselshell country, and the independence of ranch living. Never complaining, she made the best of every situation, did more than her share of work, and kept her office operating efficiently.

This day, she worked ahead of her schedule, hopefully, to please her "spoiled brat" supervisor. Her list of budgeted items would be completed well before he requested them. She had until midweek to finish the complex list. To meet competition the railroad was upgrading the dining car service to provide the same experience of luxury hotels. The multi-purpose service afforded a buffet lounge, a place to eat good food with elaborate place settings. Private sleeping compartments were available to those who could afford to travel in comfort. It was her and her associates' job to assure the rolling hotels had a generous inventory to appease First-Class passengers.

As she glanced at the big clock in the hall, she realized it was almost time to meet Toby. She had no knowledge of the tasks of his next assignment or the journey he was about to begin. Any meeting with Toby usually produced surprises.

This day was too beautiful to waste wrestling numbers. She picked up her sweater and strode out into the sunshine.

Three

The maître d' of their favorite restaurant seated Toby and Julie near the entry. It was good for business to seat the best-looking couples near the front, thus adding status and the appearance of class to the establishment. The pair drew admiring glances from all classes.

Conversation was slow and Julie could tell Toby was laboring with something unusually important on his mind. It wasn't until they were seated at the hotel table that Julie asked, "You aren't your cheery self. What is it that's bothering you?"

Toby sighed and replied, "I have to go back out west to find out what's happening to our cattle shipments."

Julie raised a perfect eyebrow and asked, "You've been bothered with this before, so what is it now?"

Toby explained, "The cattle brokers are putting their cattle aboard the trains for shipment to Chicago, or a few other processing plants along the route. But when the stock is inventoried at the destination, the count is all too frequently less than it was on the manifest. In other words, cattle are disappearing from the train somewhere en route. The N.P. (Northern Pacific Railroad) has to reimburse the brokers for the loss. And you know how serious top management is about cutting expenses and losses."

Julie continued her inquiry, "I thought we had the Pinkerton Company on retainer to provide security for our freight. Why can't they figure it out?"

Toby's response was, "It's not that easy. Here we are a state, but further west politics and law enforcement are still rather loosely organized. None of those areas are states yet. So there's Oregon Territory, Montana Territory, and Dakota Territory. Not even Pinkerton can coordinate an investigation between the different agencies, and none of them have the resources to devote time to our little problem. Pinkerton is not strong on investigations, especially on in-house matters. It appears this is due to something, or someone in the company. Our division Vice President, Mr. Hanson, wants this figured out and corrected right away, and of course, he always leans on me. He figures I can nose around in our cattle terminals and identify the problem."

"What about Eddy? He knows all the guys working the stock at the rest stations."

"I will spend a day in Miles City with Eddy on the way to Spokane, but according to Eddy's telegrams, he has no idea what can be happening to the cattle. We are going to try to work out some reliable way to count the cattle in route so that we can get an idea where they are disappearing."

Julie smiled and opined, "Well you know Eddy. He sees a lot, and says nothing. Eddy's a rounder but surely, he would never steal anything. I just can't vision Eddy as a thief."

Toby responded quickly, "I know that Eddy is a trickster and an extraordinary deal maker, but I trust him completely. Whatever is happening, I don't believe Eddy has anything to do with it. Although, I am a little disappointed that he hasn't been able to help me with the problem. It's clear that he just doesn't have a clue."

"How many cattle are you missing?"

"So far the NP has paid for sixty- five beef cattle, fifteen hogs, and 20 sheep."

"Wow!" Julie exclaimed. "How come they are disappearing in groups of five?"

"Good question", Toby pondered.

"Also, who are the brokers? Are there lots of them, or just a few? Are there any of the same people incurring the losses?"

The conversation was halted when the waiter came to take their order. Both ordered soup with a sandwich. Toby asked for coffee and Julie ordered tea with sugar and milk. The pause gave Toby time to consider her last question.

"You know, that's a great point. I haven't been able to see the original records and compare all the names of the shippers and the people making the claims. I will be able to do that when I get to Spokane. I already have the statements of loss, but I still have to get the names."

Julie smiled, "That shouldn't take you too long. Why do you even have to go out there to get them? Can't they send you the information?"

"They could, but because it looks like it might involve someone in the NP, I don't know who to trust. The moment I start prying into the records, it will probably tip off the people in question."

Julie just wouldn't let it drop. "So you think it is a records thing and that cattle are not really missing?"

Toby paused as if he wanted to be done talking about it. "I just don't know how someone could remove that many animals from our train cars. Our guys are out there caring for every shipment, and it would take a pretty big conspiracy to sneak away so many."

The waiter brought their plates and the conversation changed.

Julie spoke with a happier, but still inquiring tone, "So when do you think you will be back?"

Toby had been thinking about just how he was going to answer this anticipated question. "Well, there's one more thing I have to do on this trip."

Julie raised her eyebrow again but looked at him silently.

He continued, "You know that they play a lot of poker in the club cars." He saw Julie nod and continued, "We have had several complaints that professional gamblers are fleecing the cattlemen in the games. Apparently, there is one particular group that seems to have a system of cheating and the victims are blaming the NP for allowing crooks to prey on them. It's very bad for public relations and once again Pinkerton has been reluctant to get involved. So as I travel, I will have to linger around the stations or take short rides until I can identify who appears to be the offending gamblers."

This time, Julie was more animated and sarcastically stated, "Dearly beloved Toby. I know that you are an enormously talented superman among humans, but how does Mr. Hanson think that little Toby Hawthorn is going to bust up a poker game among cut-throats, cattle thieves and, (with a smile) bull shippers, confiscate their ill gained booty, and redistribute it to their destitute wives and starving little children scattered across the mountains and plains of this checkered society. Does he think God rides in your pocket?"

Toby grinned at her response and countered with, "No, my dearest. It is I who ride in God's pocket."

They both burst out laughing and Toby took her hand. "Don't worry. All I am going to do is observe and verify or confirm the activity and report the details to management who will decide what to do."

They had finished their lunch, and the waiter presented Toby with the bill. Two bowls of soup at ten cents each, and two sandwiches at ten cents each plus coffee and tea at five cents for a total of fifty cents caused Toby to place a fifty-cent piece on the bill and a dime tip to the side.

He leaned back in his chair and wistfully stated, "I wish my boarding house served food this good. But I guess I shouldn't complain because their room and board rates are reasonable."

Julie asked, "What do you have to pay them each month?"

Toby explained, "They just increased it from five seventy-five to six dollars a month."

Julie replied, "Thank goodness I can live with my aunt. I share with the groceries and help her with her chores, but it saves a lot of money." She paused and said wistfully, "When she expires, she will leave me her house, but I don't know how I will maintain that big place."

Toby looked at her quietly and said, "We're both twenty years old. Perhaps we should get married. We could join in the task."

Julie stared at him, and bit her lower lip before speaking. "Toby, how long have we been best friends?"

"Forever, or at least since we were little kids."

"Well", she paused, "I can't get married."

"What?"

"No one has asked me."

"Huh?"

"Tobias, no one has asked me to get married."

"Well I guess that's good, but I don't understand!"

"If you want to marry me, you have to ask me if I will do so!"

Toby's face was blank, as if his mind had been removed and replaced with cold lard. Then suddenly the sharp pins within Julie's wit penetrated his jelled conscience and he exclaimed, "Oh, my God, of course. Julie, I love you. Will you marry me?"

Before he could speak again, Julie got out of her chair, proceeded around the small table and kissed him directly on the lips. Many in the restaurant looked on while she kissed his forehead a second time. A middle-aged gentleman seated across the room loudly exclaimed, "I don't know what he had for lunch, but I'll have some of it too."

The room erupted in laughter. Toby blushed, stood up and bowed in the direction of the man and took Julie's hand while they walked out onto the street.

Four

Sunday had passed quickly. Monday May thirty-first at, six AM Toby boarded the NP westward bound passenger train. He would first meet with Eddy Kingston in Miles City, and continue on to Spokane, in Oregon Territory. He had sent letters asking Eddy to set up some kind of system where he could verify the count of all the cattle being shipped through Miles City. Because of the way the invoicing was done, he knew the shortages were only occurring within shipments between Spokane in Oregon Territory and Bismarck, in Dakota Territory. A large administrative office in Spokane recorded all livestock transportation initiating between there and Bismarck. He was not acquainted with the majority of personnel at the lower levels of the livestock business and he would have to rely on Eddy to help direct his inquiry. His train carriage moved slowly with many stops along the way, allowing ample time for his records review and planning.

Toby was already thinking about his secondary mission. He needed to identify the professional gamblers who were cheating the cattle brokers in poker. It was too early in the day to visit the club car, so he relaxed in his plush coach seat and contemplated the past weekend.

He had long thought of marrying Julie. But neither were in a financial position to support more than themselves, and unable to "set up" a household. She had come from a much more affluent family; her father a Montana rancher and her aunt a prominent St. Paul resident. Her widowed mother presumably was still owner of the Montana ranch, but had died recently while living with her sister, Aunt Rosie. Julie was a hard-working young lady, but had a less desperate future outlook, other than at her age, society expected most women to be married.

Toby realized that he had been shy and slow to ask for her hand, but after this weekend, he was mentally distracted with an entire world of new plans…all yet to be formed.

*****

Seven-hundred miles to the west, Eddy Kingston was up early. He sat on the top fence rail of the Pioneer Stock Yards corral in Miles City. The corrals were situated very close to the fort on land formerly controlled by the Army. The government designated one-hundred square miles, or sixty-four thousand acres in the jurisdiction of Fort Keogh. Land was then given to the town that grew up next to the fort. The town took the name of General Miles, and the NP railroad was instrumental in supplying the fort. As he looked toward the Yellowstone River, only a few yards to the north he could also see the confluence of the Tongue River as it twisted up from the south.

Eddy was worried. For almost five years he had been working for the NP, helping manage cattle transportation. It was a comfortable position, and the job had gone smoothly. Through steady and reliable work he had become the boss of several cattle shipping and rest stations between Livingston and Bismarck. His informal management style had won him the admiration of local cattlemen, residents and brokers throughout the business. But now there was a problem and NP officials were looking directly at him as if he could be part of it. Worst of all, he had no idea what was causing the cattle shortages.

Toby Hawthorn would be arriving from St. Paul tomorrow. Toby was expecting him to have a method of counting all the cattle that came through his territory, which Toby thought could be done at his Miles City station. He doubted that Toby realized how difficult it was to count each animal.

Every small town that shipped freight had a depot and a depot agent. But each agent only reported and kept track of freight shipped through their own depot. Many depots had cattle pens for shipping or rest areas. However, Eddy was successful in convincing the NP to combine the rest areas into four major ones; Livingston, Billings, Miles City, and Bismarck. Eddy was the central figure who now had to provide a count to identify the "leak". Toby was a long-time friend, but Eddy knew he was a serious NP employee and he did not want to disappoint him.

Eddy was deep in thought, and didn't hear his name being called. A dark-haired skinny kid of ten years approached the fence and shouted, "Hey Eddy, are you asleep on the fence?"

Eddy turned to see one of his young neighborhood friends. "Timmy, I haven't seen you in a couple of days. Where's your two buddies?"

"Aw shucks, I'm bummin'-round by myself today. Chubby's mom always washes clothes on Mondays, and she makes him help. He has to hang up the cloths 'cause Chubby's dad put the clothes line up high so the sheets don't drag on the ground. But Chubby's mom is short and can't reach high enough to fasten the clothes. Chubby is just as short, but he stands on a bucket. His mom won't use the bucket 'cause she's sort of fat, and has trouble jumping up on the bucket. Chubby's fat too, but when he falls, he don't hurt nothin'. So Chubby has to help most Mondays.

And Joe's mom is make'n him stay at home today because yesterday he went swimming in the river in the morning when he wasn't supposed to. But he really didn't go swimming, 'cause he was fishing and got the old bolt he was using for a sinker caught in the rocks about ten feet from shore. He didn't have no more bolts or sinkers of any kind, or even any more hooks, so he took off his clothes and waded out and saved the line without breaking it. But he kept his shoes on, and made the mistake of going home with them wet. All of our moms say we can only swim in the afternoons, so she said he had to stay home 'till Wednesday. But Joe's dad likes the fish he catches, so he stuck up for him, and now he only has to stay home today. Joe's dad is OK, but his grandpa is sort of mean."

As Timmy paused, Eddy questioned, "Why do you think he's mean?"

Timmy rambled on with his typically wordy dialogue. "Well, Joe's grandpa spends a lot of time out in his back yard shed. He builds things out there. One time I was in the shed talking with him and asked why he had three round holes in the bottom of the shed door. He said, 'I have three cats.' That sounded weird, so I asked why he needed a hole for each cat. He said, 'When I say scat, I mean scat.' I thought that was kind of mean, but Joe says his grandpa is always joking and the holes were really made when the shed was used as a smoke house. But still, I don't know when he's saying stuff for real or if he is joking, so he sometimes scares me."

Eddy laughed and said, "I think you just need to get to know him better."

Timmy fell silent for a moment. His facial expression changed. He had a unique way of tucking his lower lip under his upper front teeth and frowning when in deep thought. Then he brightened into a smile. His eyes met Eddy's again and he responded.

"Well I know he jokes a lot 'cause last summer when it was so hot and dry, he said he saw a coyote chasing a rabbit and it was so hot they were both walking. Now I know that's not true, but when he says it, he looks right at you without smiling and makes you think it is true, and I'm afraid to laugh because I don't want to make him mad if it's real."

The youngster hopped up onto the fence and sat beside Eddy. He looked up at Eddy and inquired, "Did my mom come and see you again?"

"No Timmy, why would she visit me again?"

"Well, remember when Chubby hurt his arm and you told us we couldn't ride the cows in the corral anymore? Well, I know that was the first time she came to see you because she wanted to be sure you knew that we were having what she thought was 'too much fun' up here at the corrals. But you didn't tell us we couldn't ride the hogs and so we kept doing that 'cause you saw us and didn't get mad. But then I came home with pig poop all over my pants. She knew right away what it was 'cause that stuff smells even worse than the goose poop down by the river. She wanted to know how that happened. I had to tell her the truth 'cause I didn't want to get into more trouble for fibbing. So now she says she is going to come back and talk to you about it again. She was mad about the pig poop, but didn't seem to be too mad about coming back up here, 'cause she said you were a nice man."

"Timmy, I was really busy when I saw you boys riding the hogs, and I didn't have time to talk to you about it. I was very concerned, and what worried me most was this: Some of those hogs have been raised eating meat, like dead cows and horses. If you fall in front of one of those big ones, they could gobble up a chunk of you before you knew something was missing. So let me say it again. You guys, all of you, have to quit riding the stock here. That means cows, calves, sheep and hogs. If it keeps up, either you boys or the cattle are going to get hurt. So if you guys want to remain my friends, you have to do what I think is best for all of us. Now, if your mom wants to come talk to me again, I will be pleased to see her."

"I'll bet she comes. She asked me a lot of questions about you."

"Timmy, where do you live? You always seem to come up from down by the river."

"Her and me live down in those cottonwoods by the river in a little house that used to be my grandpa's. She's not married and not really my mom. She is my real mom's little sister. My mom died from smallpox when I was six. I don't know what happened to my dad, they never tell me. He was a soldier from Fort Keogh."

"I guess that explains a few things. Timmy what grade are you in?"

"This fall I am going to be in the fifth grade. Chubby is going to be there with me, but Joe will be in the sixth."

"So do you like arithmetic? How far can you count? Can you count into the hundreds?"

"Mr. Eddy, I can count from now until everybody in this town is fast asleep, and when I drop off, I can start again where I shut down."

"How about your buddies, Joe and Chubby? And can you count fast?"

"Sure, we play hide and seek, and you have to count to fifty when you're it, and have to hide your eyes when you count before you go find whoever's hide'n. You have to count out loud to prove you aren't cheat'n, but every one of us can count in a blur."

"I have an idea how you, and maybe the other boys could help me here at the stock yard. I need to count all the animals that come into the corrals for the next few days."

"All of them?"

"Yep."

"Jeepers Eddy! Those pigs run around like ants on honey. And the sheep all look the same. Sometimes it's hard to tell their heads from their butts. They come off the cars like a water fall. How we gonna do that?'

"Well Timmy, the part of the sheep that's moving downhill or to open spaces is usually the head. The part that's usually hiding the nose of another sheep is the butt. I think we can fix a chute that will squeeze them down to single or double file, and if you are good enough to count them, like in twos or fives, I mean five at a time, you could count two-hundred or more without a problem."

"It would sure be fun trying."

"Timmy, the best part is that I would be willing to pay you five cents an hour, or if you have help, a total of ten cents an hour for the time you spend working up here. But you have to understand, playing around won't count."

"Wow, five cents an hour! When can I start?"

"First we'll have to get your mom's permission. Is it OK to call her your mom, or your aunt?"

"I call her mom, because everybody should have a mom, and she treats me like her son. She works over at Fort Keogh, but not far from here and I am going to tell her to come see you right away."

"OK, Timmy, I would like to get this set up before sunup tomorrow. If she can't come today, would you come back and tell me. Then perhaps I could come to your house this evening after work."

"Good, Eddy, I can run all the way to where she works without stopping. I can be there and back in less than an hour."

Timmy was out of sight before Eddy had entered his office. His first task was to get the work staff to construct the chutes needed to slow the animals as they entered the corrals for their rest stop. His plan was to count the animals both exiting, and re-entering the cattle cars, for a double count confirmation. He had some doubts about the boys, but he had no personnel to spare, or who were capable of counting animals for several days in a row. But Eddy felt good about his decision. He liked the boys. He knew he had been too lax in disciplining them to prevent their riding the animals, but initially he saw little harm in their fun. The NP would definitely not approve, but Eddy remembered when he was age ten. Now in his mid-twenties, he was unmarried, adventuresome and still full of life.

Timmy did not return within the hour as Eddy expected. His concern mounted until mid-afternoon when he saw Timmy in the company of his "mom" approaching his work shed. The young lady was modestly attired in a plain blue dress. Her attractiveness did not come from her clothing, but from her shiny dark hair, clear tanned skin, delicate features and shy smile. Timmy was not dressed in his usual ragged jeans and tee shirt, but instead wore newly washed pants and a short-sleeved shirt.

As Eddy stepped out of the shed, the lady humbly spoke, "Hello! Remember me? I'm Alice Horton, Tim's Aunt. I understand you wanted to speak with me. I must say upfront that if Timmy has gotten into trouble again, we sincerely apologize."

Eddy laughed, "Hey, he's a good kid. I enjoy seeing him and his buddies. I wanted to talk to you about making them a deal; something to do other than ride the cattle."

Alice's eyes widened and said, "Timmy said something about paying him to count cattle?"

"Yes, he seems like a bright kid, and I need someone to help us count the livestock here for the next few days. The railroad can afford to pay for the help, and I offered him five cents an hour, and up to ten cents if he gets help from his friends. He can decide how much to pay his friends because there are two of them, and we can't pay three separate wages."

"Really Mr., ah, I've only heard you called Eddy."

"Eddy Kingston miss."

"Thank you, Mr. Kingston. I was going to say your offer is very generous. It is, and we sincerely appreciate it. But you should understand that I work at the fort four days a week and Timmy would be responsible for his own appearance at the times you desire. I fear for the reliability of his timeliness."

Eddy immediately liked this attractive, quiet spoken little lady. This was his second meeting with her and he found the reoccurrence surprisingly pleasant. He displayed his best manners.

"Miss Horton, I think we can work out a system to have him respond when needed. We don't have cattle here every single day. Then sometimes we have hundreds in and out in just a few hours. We won't count on Sundays. I understand you live by the river near here?"

"Yes, down by the cottonwoods over where the Tongue dumps into the Yellowstone."

Eddy continued in his charming manner, "If agreed, Tim could come meet us around seven in the morning on week days at which time we would know when we would be loading or unloading stock. We operate by railroad time around here, so we know pretty close what time the stock trains come in. Maybe if I look around, we could even find an old railroad watch to loan him."

As Eddy finished his sentence mentioning the watch, he winked at Alice. She blushed and looked toward the ground for a few short seconds. When she recovered, she said, "Mr. Kingston, you may call me Alice. We are most grateful and I am sure Timmy will pester you until his very first count begins. I wish you both luck after that."

Eddy slapped his jeans with his right hand, dusting it off, and extended the partly clean palm to the lady, saying, "I'll call you Alice only if you call me Eddy. We will be sure to look after Timmy while he does our counting. And I hope I will see you again."

Alice smiled shyly, took Eddy's hand in a delicate shake, and said, "That would be a pleasure."

Five

Eddy met Toby at the NP rail station. He was driving a hack owned by the NP, powered by two matched Percheron horses. Eddy owned a saddle horse, but only one, and the NP expected to transport their customers and staff in comfort. Although they were old friends, Eddy greeted Toby with guarded respect. The first few minutes were awkward.

"Toby, it's good to see you. Sorry you are here on a mission of trouble…or should I say to get us out of trouble."

"Hello Eddy. Hey friend, we are not in trouble yet. We just need to figure out who is causing our trouble."

"Sure, do we need to go to a hotel first, or are you leaving…or I guess the next passenger train isn't until tomorrow morning. Where do you want to stay?"

Toby recognized Eddy's discomfort and smiled. "I can stay at the NP boarding house for tonight. We should be able to work up a plan today so that I can get on to Billings tomorrow."

Eddy turned the horses toward the west, and it was Toby who spoke next.

"You need to know that these shortages are an embarrassment to all of us, but no one believes you are at fault. When management sees losses which are probably theft, they put the candle under everyone's behind until they get answers. Eddy, you and I are going to figure this out."

The hack rattled noisily toward the west making it hard to hear conversation. Toby silently observed the rapid changes in the growing town. As they approached the bridge crossing the Tongue River, Toby asked, "Is this the bridge that has fallen down twice?"

Eddy replied, "Yup, it collapsed in Eighty-One, and again in Eighty-Three while cattle were crossing. Fifty of them fell into the river. The fort plans to build a steel one next year."

"Is that why so many soldiers walk to town over the railroad bridge?"

Eddy was becoming more relaxed. He answered, "And that continues to be a problem. They walk to town, get drunk and on the way back fall off the bridge into the river. The bridge has no side rails; why should it, it's a railroad bridge. It's tricky to keep your feet on the ties. A couple had to jump off when a train without a working headlight crossed at night. No one has been killed yet, but that's one of the reasons the fort wants to build a good bridge over here."

In another five minutes they arrived at Eddy's stockyard office. The small talk was over.

Eddy cleared the office of any other personnel and the discussion began. Toby recognized Eddy was back to his old self when he said, "OK Bub. How we gonna handle this?"

"Eddy, I am breaking from the preferred plan here because for this to work, none of the people working at the cattle rest stations can know about it. So from right now, all of this is confidential. A lot of management thinks there is some type of theft ring operating at the rest stops, but I don't believe it for several reasons. First of all, it is too difficult to secretly move that many animals out of the corrals without someone seeing what's happening. It would mean at least half of the station employees would be participating in the thefts. Secondly, the cattle are disappearing in groups of fives. That appears to me to be a stroke of the pen, rather than someone hauling away animals in a wagon that is just the right size to fit five head at a time."

Toby continued, "My plan is to have you, and the Billings station, do a count of every head passing through. I don't expect that your counts will always match perfectly, because live and moving cattle are hard to count. But your numbers shouldn't differ more than one or two, and certainly they won't differ in amounts of five. So what I am thinking is that if you and the Billings station independently verify the count, and if it's less than invoiced in Spokane, the shortage is occurring before the shipment gets to the Yellowstone Division. In other words, the theft is occurring at Spokane or maybe in Spokane's paperwork, or somewhere between Spokane and Billings. And guess what Eddy, most of the trains don't stop between Billings and Spokane other than to load other items. If small shipments of cattle are put aboard at the smaller depots they are placed on special separate invoices and railed to Billings in smaller trains."

Toby relaxed a moment and studied Eddy, who was nodding his head almost imperceptibly. Toby leaned over the table toward Eddy and spoke even more softly. "I'm going to look at the books in Spokane, and if they show more animals are aboard than Billings or your count, then we are going to fire whoever holds the pen out there, and find out what the connection is with the people collecting money from the NP for fake losses. We have been paying cattle shippers for these losses, but when I went over the payments, I noticed all the payments went to just three brokers. I intend to find out who they are and where they come from."

Toby handed Eddy a half sheet of paper containing three names. "Have you ever heard of these guys in your territory?"

Eddy studied the names before he replied, "The first two don't mean anything to me, but the last one there on the bottom is unusual and I remember something about it. I think the name Bossmiller belongs to a guy that comes through here regularly. No one calls him by his real name, they just refer to him as "Big B." He is supposed to be a cattle broker, but he also seems to be a big gambler. I know that, because I was with some of the soldiers at the fort a few months ago and they were moaning about losing money to him. As you probably know, the NP gives transportation tickets to the Army people here at the fort for half price, so the troops can get away on leave.

Apparently, this guy Bossmiller has lifted more than one of their pay checks playing poker."

Toby sat back straight in his chair. "That's interesting, really interesting! I have also been asked to look into a crooked gambling operation taking place in the club cars. This gets better as we go. Maybe cattle thievery and poker thievery go together, and the NP is being used as the facilitator. What's this guy they call Big B guy look like?"

"He's an ugly bugger with a big nose and a pox marked face. But he dresses like a big shot. I'd guess he's about forty years old, big, maybe six feet plus and tips the scales to at least two-hundred-fifty pounds; I mean soft puffy pounds. I don't know if the B in 'Big B' stands for butt, belly, or something even worse. He always wears a hat, but his hair is dark brown, with lots of it hanging down near his collar. He smokes cigars, wears heavy boots and usually a vest."

Toby sat silent for a few moments, as if he was locking details into his mental safe. "That's good information. I'll watch for him. Eddy, do you have any questions or comments about the problem or plan?"

Eddy shook his head, saying, "No."

Toby asked, "What have you got set up to count the stock?"

Eddy was dreading this question, and was hoping it wasn't asked. He knew he had to answer it straight and defend his position.

"Well, you know that our budget here won't allow for hiring expensive help, and you also told me to do this quietly. There are two and sometimes three boys who like to hang around here. They are good kids and have demonstrated to me they are capable of doing the count. I figure hiring them on the cheap, and getting two or three individual independent counts would be what we need."

Toby interrupted with, "That sounds good, but why do they hang around here?"

Eddy thought to himself, Oops, now I've done it. Toby's too alert to miss anything.

Then he commented out loud, "Well, the truth is I caught them riding the cows. They were sitting up on the top rails of the fence and when a doggie passed close by, they would jump on for a ride. Some of the little devils were good riders. But I had to put an end to their fun before they or the cattle got hurt. I figured it was better to make friends with them and have them want to please me rather than be mean to them and have additional problems. The kids were good about it, so I let them continue to come up and watch us work the cattle. I spoke to one of the parents. She was very friendly and with everyone working together, we stopped the rodeo."

Eddy looked at Toby for a response and was surprised at the reaction.

Toby grinned saying, "Let me get this straight. The NP is losing its butt in the cattle business and you hired three kids to bail us out; but it's OK because they're good calf riders. That's funny." Then after a long tense pause, "But Eddy we know and trust each other. So if that's your plan, I'll go with it. Just don't tell the NP we're using kids to rescue the company. I think they may have forgotten surveyor Teel hired me on my 15th birthday. Did you clear this with the parents, and what did you have to tell them?"

"I put the brightest and best kid in charge. I have spoken with his mom who seems quite happy with the arrangement."

"How old are these kids?"

"Timmy, the boss is in the fifth grade along with his buddy Chubby. The other, Joe ,will be in the sixth, so I think they are eleven and twelve."

Toby stood up and said, "OK pardner, it's your show from here. But I have some time to kill before tomorrow so why don't we look around to see how you are going to slow down these critters so the kids can count them."

They went out into the sunshine and to the docking ramp where the cattle were unloaded. Eddy explained, "We separate the stock of course. Sheep and pigs go into the pens with the low railings, beef cattle and horses go off to the west in the taller fences. We can narrow the entry gates and give the boys a platform to sit on and count as they go by."

Toby injected, "You'll have to be careful that they don't crush each other in a stampede to get out of the rail cars."

"Yah, we thought of that and will have someone regulate their rate getting out of the cars. We can open the doors only slightly so they don't all try to get out at once."

Eddy was happy to explain what he had worked out. "After the stock have been fed and watered, and the rest period is over, we can run them back into the cars, with the boys recounting them on the way back in."

Toby was satisfied. "That looks good to me. Whenever you have all three of the boys working, that will give us six actual counts of each shipment and heaven knows it should tell us how many head we have."

The tension was off and they both sat down on feed buckets next to the grain bins. Toby said, "I keep thinking about that guy Big B. Is there anything else you can tell me about him?" Does he go into town, or come out here to look at the stock? Where did you see him?"

Eddy replied, "I only saw him once. My friend Jim Young Bear, you know, from the Crow Tribe, and I were in a little sandwich place near the Depot " - -

Toby interrupted, "Oh, yes, Jim, I hadn't forgotten about him. Has he returned from the gold fields?"

"Yes, he's now working at the sawmill here in Miles City."

"Anyway, Big B came in with a couple of cowboys. He stood out because he was dressed different. One of the guys who works with me and drinks with the Army crowd pointed him out; said he was a big wheeler dealer and traveled all over the West. I can't really say much more about him, other than he looked pretty soft. If he was cheating them, I'm surprised the soldiers haven't roughed him up. I guess they have to stay out of trouble. He looked big, but I could have him on the ground in ten seconds."

Toby chided, "I thought you gave up fighting."

"I did, but when you see a guy that desperately needs the crap pounded out of him, it causes you to at least think about it."

"Um-hm, sometimes Julie says the same thing about her boss. He's a little wimp that thumps his chest and orders the ladies around like only he was maintaining their existence."

Eddy asked, "Oh yes, how's life in St. Paul? Are you and Julie still best friends?"

Toby grinned, "I guess you might say that. Two days ago I asked her to marry me."

Eddy yelped, "Fantastic! I'm guessing she said yes."

"She sure did, and as soon as I get back, we are going to make plans for a ceremony this month."

"Well, if there's a celebration, count me in as guest number one."

"Eddy, you're always number one."

After a minute of happy laughter, Toby asked, "What about you? Are you still seeing that little red head Grace?"

"Nope, but I see her now and then, dating her soldier friend. We weren't riding the same path, so we just parted friends."

"That's too bad. But a guy like you should not have trouble making friends, especially with the ladies."

"Funny you should say that, because there seems to be a mutual interest between me and Timmy's mom."

Surprised, Toby questioned, "Really, how old is she? She must be a lot older than you if she comes with an eleven-year-old kid!"

"Not really. Timmy is actually her older sister's boy. His real mother died of smallpox a few years ago, and his father was killed somehow while in the Army. Timmy is a good kid, and anyway, I am going to explore the situation. In the brief time I have known her, she has been very good company. I'm going slow cause I don't want to mix business with pleasure." Toby laughed at his uncharacteristic caution.

The remainder of the day passed quickly as the two friends renewed their bond. Toby needed to return to town for the evening and prepare for the rest of his journey the next day. Eddy volunteered, "Do you want me to hook up the hack, or can you still ride in a saddle?"

Toby commented, "Actually I would rather travel on something that eats grass and wears hair, than all the contraptions I have been on lately."

Eddy rode with Toby into town, and returned home with both his and the company horse. He looked up at the dimming sunset and thought, "Sometimes you have to wait until evening to see how splendid the day has been."

Six

The June third NP Express passenger train carried Toby out of Miles City early. He was pleased with his visit and arrangements with Eddy. He proceeded along the aisles of the coach cars in route to the dining car. It was his intention to have a good breakfast and enjoy the club car all the way to Billings. As he entered the dining car, his attention was immediately drawn toward a large man at the far end. Toby took a seat on the opposite end of the car that would allow him to inconspicuously watch the passenger. The big guy fit the description provided by Eddy. This train originated in Miles City, so the man either transferred from the westbound Bismarck train, or got on at Miles City. Toby ordered breakfast and casually watched the big fellow. He was dressed in brown pants, white pin striped shirt and a brown vest. He had to be the cattle broker/gambler, bearing a big nose, pox marks and large girth.

Twenty minutes later he was joined by another person, appearing to be a cowboy. Toby studied the second man with the feeling he had encountered him previously. After several minutes of observance he realized the cowboy was wearing a neckerchief inappropriately, indoors during a warm June morning. If his memory was correct, he suspected the cowboy was covering up a significant scar on his neck. It would be the scar he received from Eddy Kingston's boot five years ago in the Montana Territory town of Coulson, next to Billings. The Cowboy was a little heavier and more weathered, but strongly resembled the past foe. If he was the same person, Toby was certain that the cowboy would soon recognize him because he too had an unfriendly encounter with the man. Toby decided to stay in place and see what happened. Toby didn't realize how much his own appearance had changed in five years. He had changed from a boy of fifteen to a sizable man of twenty. For more than an hour, Toby went unnoticed.

The pair finally moved to the club car which was further toward the rear of the train. As the cowboy was leaving the dining car, he surveyed the passengers and for a brief moment locked onto Toby. Not to be intimidated, Toby met his eyes with a firm gaze and the man turned and proceeded out of the car, leaving Toby with no definite conclusions.

After observing the cowboy for most of an hour, Toby was relatively sure he was the man whom he and Eddy only referred to as "Scar-neck." The Coulson incident was not easy to forget. As a result of an argument originated by Scar-neck's thievery, Eddy's boot found the cowboy's neck, causing serious injury, finalized by Eddy and Toby spending the night in jail. This had to be the same man, and now he seemed to be associated with another suspected villain, Mr. Big B.

Toby waited another half an hour before entering the club car. It was only mid-morning and the car was sparsely occupied. Big B and Scar-neck were already drinking liquor. The latter was leaning back in his lounge chair as if he were about to doze off, while Big B sat at a table with a deck of cards spread out, appearing to be playing solitaire. Toby interpreted this as an open enticement for someone to join him in a game. What kind of a game? Knowing the reputation of the man, it would be some type of "I'll play, you pay."

Toby, not a drinker, stayed only long enough to read the travelers newspaper, and seeing the pair were not engaged in any activity, returned to the observation coach.

The NP express train traveled an average of thirty-five miles per hour. It was much faster and preferred over stage coach or horse and buggy. The trip to Billings was going to take at least four hours, meaning he would arrive about midday. He did not anticipate that the gamblers would gather at the poker table until after lunch. He realized he would have to observe the participants at another time during this journey. He doubted Big B and his sidekick would travel west much beyond Spokane. He had hopes of encountering them in the coming week.

Toby got off the NP Express at the Billings Depot. It was less than a mile walk to the stockyards. He made arrangements with the Depot Agent to store his personal luggage and walked to the NP cattle yards that were shared with a local meat processing company.

As Toby approached the facility, he observed how easy it would be to "misdirect" a few animals into the corrals of the slaughter house instead of the resting and feeding pens. But if that was occurring, it would now be immediately noticed as a result of the new counting system. Eddy had insisted the NP crew in Billings were honest and competent. Eddy had a special talent in recognizing human character and Toby did not doubt his judgment.

This meeting would be brief. The Billings crew had already been told they were to begin a new method of accountability and that Toby would arrive to explain the details. Toby intended only to review their system and personally advise the crew to keep the new counting procedures confidential.

When he entered the stockyard office, Toby found most of the crew was expecting him. He regretted that they had not been cautioned to keep his visit confidential, but since they didn't know the purpose of his visit, his mission was not compromised. It was not uncommon for headquarters officials to check on field operations. Toby made a few suggestions, taking ideas from Eddy in Miles City. None of the employees had a plausible explanation for the stock shortages other than insisting they were not responsible. Most were insulted, and took it personally, that they were even considered as a possible source of theft. Toby thanked them for their participation and returned to the

Depot. It was late in the day. He retrieved his belongings and retired to a hotel nearby.

Friday, June fourth, Toby boarded the Westbound NP Express for Spokane. This would be the longest leg of his journey. He expected to arrive late on June fifth, after traveling all night. He enjoyed the scenery as they entered the Rocky Mountains and stopped briefly in Livingston and Bozeman. The familiar territory, spoke to him as if ghosts in the clouds were sending whispering breezes, speaking in language only he could understand. They were telling him he belonged here with them. The experience renewed his inner struggle between the economics of existence and the desire of an independent soul to be free in the wilderness. He vowed to someday regain that freedom, but for now, suppressed it by concentrating on the expectations of St. Paul.

Across the continental divide, the train stopped at Butte, still in Montana Territory. Butte was a regular stop to transfer mail and light freight, even if there were no passengers boarding or departing. Toby was lightly dozing in his plush coach seat, when his senses were awoken by a familiar frame entering the car. It was the hulk of Big B. Following close behind was Scar-neck. They had apparently spent the previous evening in Butte. Toby slumped unnoticed as they passed by. He wondered why they would spend the night in Butte. It was not a cattle station, but was well known for mining and smelting at nearby Anaconda. Toby theorized that because Butte was a popular town for good whisky, night life and gambling, the pair of scoundrels may have worked their trade by "mining" the miners. The available information indicated that Big B was the gambler working the NP passenger line, and Toby was unable to imagine what role Scar-neck had in the operation. One thing was a certainty. If the two were traveling together, they were working together. Both were men of bad reputation and character.

After an hour beyond Butte, Toby walked into the dining cars, looked over the passengers and determined the two men had gone to the club car at the rear of the train. He decided to leave them unobserved until evening, not wanting to be too obvious in his surveillance.

A light meal in the dining car rested uncomfortably in Toby's nervous stomach in anticipation of his next activity. He planned to position himself close to the lounge poker table; close enough to analyze the game and methods of Big B, and his disreputable sidekick. Toby didn't care if Scar-neck finally recognized him as an NP employee. He doubted it would happen, but saw no harm in their learning of security concerns. The intent of the NP was to stop the predatorial cheating. If the activity was documented, the NP would simply deny them passage.

One of Toby's assets was now becoming a handicap. His academic and religious based home schooling, isolated in the Musselshell wilderness, left him naive about the evil in many of the West's personalities. He had little understanding of the seriousness in which men of money engaged in high stakes poker.

The poker game began early, to allow several hours of action before the late June sunset. Toby had observed Big B playing solitaire previously with his own deck of cards. Although new cards were available on request, the club car porter was never summoned. The big man appeared to make certain the cards in play came from his vest pocket. The seating arrangement also seemed curious. Scar-neck was present, but not as a player. To the uninformed observer he appeared to be aloof from Big B and sat in a seat facing his friend, but back behind a couple of the other players, close enough to observe their cards if held in the hand. The possibilities of Scar-neck's assistance to Big B were obvious, causing Toby to watch for signals or secret communication between the two.

The game began normally with "gentleman" sized bets. Toby observed nothing unusual from either of his suspects. Big B was losing small amounts, boosting his opponent's confidence and spirits. After an hour, the temperament of Scar-neck changed. He no longer sat relaxed in his chair behind the participants at the poker table. He sat more erect and began observing more closely. Big B's posture also changed. He slid closer to the table so that his pocketed vest rested against the edge. He was quicker with his hands and glanced across the table at Scar-neck frequently. Toby began to see patterns and similarities to Scar-neck's physical positioning. Big B seemed to evaluate all of his cohort's movements. A tip of the hat forward and Big B raised the bet. At tip backward and he checked or folded. A hand to the chin, a rub of an eye, a scratch of the ear, all appeared to have a meaning. Toby could clearly see that Scar-neck was looking from behind, assessing the strength of the other players' cards, and using sign language to guide the big man's plays.

Big B too, worked with quick sly movements. When he dealt, he always managed to see the bottom card of the deck. On a couple of occasions, it appeared he dealt himself that bottom card, especially when he was dealing on the draw. As they worked their trade, the fortunes of the game changed. Big B began winning. As the unsuspecting stockmen's losses mounted, they increased their bets, believing their original luck would return. It didn't. As the natural light of the day faded, the dim artificial light of the club car aided the wolves in fleecing their lambs. When the evening ended, Big B had won several thousand dollars. Only one of the victims appeared to question the honesty of Big B's good fortune. Just the mention of an accidental card exposure or a "misdeal" was met with threatening hostility from Big B. When the suspecting stockman angrily rose to leave the game, Toby saw Scar-neck's hand move toward the waistband under his jacket, where Toby was sure a gun was hidden. The stockman was smart enough to leave a loser without incurring additional damage.

Toby's presence and acute attention to the game did not go unnoticed by the devil's duo. More than once, as Big B received a signal from Scar-neck, he threw a second glance at Toby. Toby's eyes moved in tandem with all of it. He never shrank from the hateful looks and only departed when the game was over. In just one session, he had sufficient information to cause the NP to take corrective action. He recognized the manner in which a man chooses to gamble, indicates his character or his lack of it.

It was NP policy that employees traveled in first-class accommodations. Toby accessed his small sleeping room in one of the Pullman "Sleeper" cars. He lay awake until late, reviewing in his mind, the events of the past few hours. He felt he had identified the source of the gambling problem. Tomorrow he hoped to resolve the cattle shortage puzzle.

Seven

Toby rested in his compartment until the train was about a half hour out of Spokane. He was dressed and sought the stimulation of a hot cup of coffee before his departure. As he rose to leave, he noticed a torn piece of paper on the floor that had apparently been slipped under the door. With the paper in his hand he studied the irregular print. *"Poker is none of your business. Stay away from the game, or you to will be the loser."* He noted that the word to should have been too, but the rest of the note was normal, written in pencil on a quarter sheet of lined paper. He knew this had to be a warning from the pair of cheaters. Now he wondered, "Did they still not know that he was an employee of the NP?" He mused that Scar-neck should have recognized him by now, unless the alcoholic fumes were disturbing his brain. Things were starting to get personal.

Toby avoided going to the dining car, but instead walked the opposite direction to the mail car. He displayed his NP credentials to enter and was then greeted by several old NP friends he had encountered during the past five years. His intent was to stay out of sight until all passengers had departed into the Spokane Depot, and exit the train just as it was about to leave. At that time the crowd would be thin and he could better detect if he was being followed. With his travel bag in hand, he stepped to the brick platform just as the steam engine blew the departure warning whistle.

It had been a lengthy stop of almost an hour. The platform and walkway were empty except for a few freight handlers. He was successful in avoiding being observed arriving in Spokane, but his action prevented his knowing where Big B and Scar-neck were. He hoped they were still on the train. Fear was not the reason for his caution, however, other than his deceased father's knife in his boot, he was unarmed, and a physical confrontation would greatly complicate matters. He remembered Julie's admonition; that God was not in his pocket. He thought about his friend Eddy. It would have been Eddy's style to return the note to Big B and make him eat it while Scar-neck was forced to watch. Now things had changed. Scar-neck carried a revolver. Toby checked his vest to make sure he still had the threatening note. It would be of use in the future.

It was quitting time at the Spokane NP office. Employees were leaving when Toby walked into the company complex. He reported to the office superintendent who supposedly was the only person who was to know of his visit. He was treated cordially and shown the area where the livestock shipping and accounting was conducted. Most documents were in unlocked file cabinets where the superintendent recommended Toby start his review. Both agreed that tomorrow, being Sunday, June sixth, the office would not be occupied, allowing him to complete his audit secretly.

The day had been eventful, but Toby did not retire to his hotel immediately. He still had a very important task to accomplish. In the boot opposite the concealed knife, he had stashed a portion of his savings for something special. That something special was to be placed on the hand of his best friend. On their wedding day, Julie would receive a gold wedding band, a symbol of their inseparable existence. He had not the time to shop in St. Paul before his departure, and was uncertain if he would have private time when he returned. It was not going to be an ordinary ring; the kind to be found in Miles City, Billings, or points in between. He was certain Spokane would have something unique. He spent the last hour before closing making his selection. He was pleased with his search. The ring was hidden where the cash had been.

The next morning, Sunday, June sixth, 1886, Toby Hawthorn, after treating himself to a plate of toast and bacon, topped off with black coffee, walked to the Spokane NP accounting offices. The back door was open as promised. The sun was brightly streaming through the tall windows, making it unnecessary to disclose his presence with additional lighting.

He opened several filing cabinets until he found the livestock shipping records. Each trainload was neatly summarized with the details attached, to include date, number of each cattle type, identity of the shipper, origin and destination. The review began with the previous several months. Toby had his own list of the shortages and compensated losses.

As he pored over the numbers, he noticed occasional corrections on the shipping documents. Each correction amounted to a small addition to the total number of cows, sheep, or hogs. Each correction was always an addition, never a subtraction. Then he searched the names of the cattle brokers to compare the corrections with the dealers reporting the losses. There were the names that claimed his attention, and made his blood leap. Carter, Vincent and Bossmiller. Each person reporting a loss had a correction on some of the shipping bills. Each name corresponded with the information provided to him by NP headquarters. These were the same names he had shown to Eddy. Toby excitedly scanned through all of the similar documents, bringing his review up to the present. He found there were no consistent corrections on each shipping document that reported losses at the destination. He then went back over the records comparing all losses with the three names. He found all losses were associated with those three brokers, and they all originated in Spokane. Even though there were not as many corrections on the accounting sheets as there were losses, Toby was certain that the numbers were being inflated by whoever was making the entries, thus giving credit to the broker for animals he had not delivered for shipment. It appeared to Toby, that the corrections were made during the beginning of the scheme, possibly as a trial to test the possibilities of the plan. After the inflationary numbers resulted in over compensation, the activity was planned in advance of the shipment documentation and corrections were not necessary.

Toby meticulously copied all of the past two weeks shipping charts. On his return East he would obtain the actual count from Billings and Miles City, knowing there were no stops to allow the removal of livestock from the train before the two rest stations. If there were differences, it would confirm his theory of corruption in the Spokane accounting office.

Toby had just finished copying the last sheet of numbers when a mature lady abruptly entered the room. She had not noticed Toby until after she closed the door, and produced an audible gasp when she turned and saw him.

Before him stood a very plain looking woman – a faded rose- who's fragrance was lost in time. She looked tired, unkept and weary of life.

"Oh!" she shuddered, "Who are you, and what are you doing here?"

Toby introduced himself and produced his NP credentials. "I'm from NP Headquarters. I'm doing routine inspection of shipping records, with special attention on livestock shipping. Is that your function in this office?"

"Well, ah, yes, this is my office. Why are you doing this on a Sunday?"

Toby answered smoothly, "Because I am here. I always work every day when I have to be away from home. Now I might ask you the same question, because I was told this office would be closed today."

She seemed to be caught by her own inquiry and stammered an answer, "I.., I was going to do some personal correspondence and I left my address book in my desk."

Toby smiled, trying to set her more at ease. "How long have you worked here?"

"About three years." As if to justify her existence, she volunteered, "I got a bookkeeping diploma from a school in Portland."

"That's good. Did you enter directly as a bookkeeper or did you have to work up to this job?"

"I started out in supply over in the maintenance shop until this job came open."

Toby continued his calm questioning, attempting to not make the conversation feel like the interrogation it was becoming.

"That was probably a happy promotion. Do they give you any help in here?"

"Yes, but Vera only does expenses and collections, and sometimes commodities or special shipping."

"What's special shipping?"

"Ah, you know, when some outfit wants to ship something very valuable or large, and the shipment needs special attention."

"Oh, of course. So do you make all the entries in the livestock accounting?"

She paused and swallowed. "Well, most of them."

"Most of them? Who else makes entries? They look to be in the same writing style."

"Ah, yah, I guess I have done all of them the last few months."

Toby gave her a disarming smile and said, "I was just noticing what nice penmanship you have. The books look very tidy. What's your name?"

"Angela, ah, Angela Johnson", she replied while fidgeting with her purse and desk drawer.

Toby saw his chance to dismiss her and said, "Well I certainly don't want to stand in the way of your personal correspondence. It was nice meeting you and I hope you have a good weekend."

Angela walked out of her office, without removing anything looking like an address book. Toby noticed that the small cardboard name plate on her desk identified her as *Angela Coulter – Livestock.*

Toby quickly jammed the accounting sheets into the file cabinets, gathered up his copies, and rushed out behind Angela. Her nervous and submissive behavior foretold she was neither the architect of this scheme, nor the energy behind it. The name Bossmiller had become omnipresent. It was essential he discover who belonged to the names being used in addition to Bossmiller. Who is Vincent and Carter? Angela obviously was disturbed by Toby's examination of the books, and terrified that her deception would be discovered. She was certain to contact her associates.

As Toby got to the street, he barely saw her back as she turned to the right one block past the NP building. He quickened his pace, not wanting to lose her. As he rounded the corner to his right, he halted and stepped back. She was only a few feet away, speaking to a man. Toby removed his hat, and peered around the corner. He recognized the man. It was Scar-neck.

Toby hesitated. If he remained just around the corner, he would be exposed if they came his direction. If he changed location, he risked losing them. His decision was to walk across the street to the left and loiter next to the window display of a clothing store.

He crossed the street and watched from a position of cover while the two talked on the street. They both seemed disturbed and animated. It appeared as though Scar-neck was giving her instructions. She did not seem to be willingly accepting his direction. She produced a handkerchief from her purse and dabbed at her eyes, apparently shedding tears. In spite of her dismay, Scar-neck was not in any manner consoling her. His fierce scowling indicated he was delivering an admonition.

Scar-neck pointed his finger at her in a parting gesture, and quickly strode away, leaving Angela between him and Toby. Unable to follow Scar-neck, Toby waited for Angela to continue her departure. She again wiped her eyes and tiredly walked toward a hive of concentrated apartments to the north.

Toby continued his observation until Angela entered one of the apartment buildings. As he walked by the building, he could see a row of mailboxes on the wall just inside the common entryway. It was almost midday, and risky to intrude so close to her dwelling, but he needed answers. He watched the building for a half an hour; long enough to see there were multiple people going in and out of the entry, which was in deep shade and dimly lit. He ventured into the entry and examined the mail boxes. The discovery was astounding.

Apparently, this was the mail collection location for several of the apartments. There were three horizontal rows of black cast iron mail boxes, similar to a post office. In the upper row appeared the name, ***Vincent***. In the second row, in the middle, he saw the name ***Angela Vincent-Coulter***. At the end of the same row he found in bold letters, ***Bossmiller***.

On discovering the moniker of "Big B", he pulled his hat low over his forehead and briskly walked out of the building toward town to emerge in the pedestrian traffic. It all was becoming apparent. Angela was either the sister or former wife of someone named Vincent. Whoever Vincent was, lived in the same apartment complex as her along with Bossmiller. With the sighting of Scar-neck in the company of both her and Bossmiller, it was probable that he was Vincent. So who was Carter?

Toby thought about the behavior of Angela. What would motivate her to cooperate with the devil's duo? Was it sheer intimidation? What was she getting out of the scheme? Why did she provide a false name when questioned? Why couldn't she give the name Angela Coulter? Was it that the name Carter was quite similar? Was she posing on paper as Carter? Toby resolved that he would have an early morning meeting with the local NP superintendent. For now he would retreat to his hotel and compose a written report of his findings.

The next morning, Tuesday, June seventh, 1886, the eastbound NP passenger train left Spokane without Toby. He was instead at the Spokane NP railroad office, waiting for the appearance of the superintendent. Precise questions had been prepared during the night, the sum of which should fill in the blanks of Toby's investigation and audit.

When the superintendent appeared, he was surprised to see Toby. "Well, good morning. I thought you would be returning to St. Paul on the morning train?"

Toby stood, and replied, "That was my intention, but some developments have raised questions that I must share with you. Perhaps you can help explain some of yesterday's observations."

The superintendent, small in stature, balding, with small round gold rimmed spectacles perched on his lower nose, rubbed his hairless scalp and flopped into his chair. With a sigh he asked, "What now?"

"Yesterday I found irregularities, in the livestock accounting, appearing in a pattern. The woman in charge of the accounting fortuitously walked in as I was auditing the books. She admitted making all of the accounting entries in the recent past, although I did not discuss specific entries or the irregularities. She appeared quite disturbed by my presence and questions and could not explain her Sunday appearance at the office. In conclusion, she departed providing me with a false name. She provided the name Angela Johnson, when her desk name tag bore the name Angela Coulter."

The superintendent stared at Toby, and could only exclaim, "Oh dear!"

Toby continued, "I would like you to confirm her name. I later observed her speaking with a man previously known to be taking advantage of the NP in a gambling operation. Although it is premature to implicate Angela in the livestock shortages, I would like to obtain as much information as possible about her. As you know, our headquarters is very intent on eliminating these losses and will go to great extent to resolve it as soon as possible. I have postponed my return, hoping that we can accomplish what needs to be done today."

The superintendent having recovered from his shock, replied with confidence, "Of course, where do we start?"

Toby explained, "We need to review her personnel file to obtain her correct name, or names. I would like to secure the last six months of livestock accounting records, for possible future evidence. If you could just lock them up here in one of your offices, that would be fine. That needs to be done as soon as possible. I don't want to give her the opportunity to change anything. Just explain that it is part of the routine audit. To add credibility to that statement, I suggest you also secure the records of the other activities within that office. I believe they are controlled by an employee named Vera. The employees should not at this point be admonished for anything, but I want each day's entries, the accounting sheets they complete, obtained and deposited with the other documents you will be securing. Do you grasp what we are trying to verify here?"

The little man leaned forward and said, "Yes Mr. Hawthorn, I understand completely. You have done a good job here in a short time. I will have the personnel file brought here immediately."

He left the room and shortly returned with a large brown envelope marked Angela Vincent, but with the name Vincent crossed out and overwritten by the last name Coulter. A memo in the file stated, "Angela was hired under the maiden name of Vincent, was thereafter married to a man with the last name Coulter who, three years ago, was subsequently killed in some sort of logging accident. She apparently had one brother whom she listed as an emergency contact."

The brother's name and address were in the file. Brother, Frank Vincent's address was the same as Angela's except for a different apartment number. Toby had identified Scar-neck. He believed that Carter was an imaginary person, invented to provide her with a share of the scheme's profits.

Toby left the superintendent's office three hours after his arrival. Satisfied with his findings, Toby reviewed his report, updated it with his latest findings and spent the afternoon enjoying a well-deserved rest. He felt a freedom from the unusual burden placed upon him and triumphant in the accomplishments of the last three days. As a final act for the day, he went to the telegraph office and sent a message to Eddy. It was short, but Eddy would understand. The message read, "JUNE 7.

CONFIDENTIAL. SHORTAGES RESOLVED. NO ACTION TAKEN YET. POSSIBLE INVOLVEMENT BY NECK AND B. CONTINUE COUNT. NO NEED FOR ADDITIONAL MEETING. RETURNING TO HQ. MORE LATER. BUB.

Tomorrow he would begin a one thousand, three-hundred-and-forty-mile trip, of four days and nights to St. Paul. The new stress would be bearing the travel burden of having nothing to do.

Eight

Julie was a happy person, usually in good spirits and optimistic. The three other women working in the office with her were strengthened by her attitude and bright personality. The last week was difficult for her. Toby had been absent for ten days. Shortly after he left for Spokane, her Aunt Rosie, who was suffering from chronic pneumonia, passed away. Her death was not unexpected, but saddened Julie greatly. Julie, whose mother died only a few months before, needed Toby for emotional support and to help with the arrangements of Rosie's internment. But because the only means of contacting him was by telegram, and because he was so far away, there was nothing he could do to help even if he was aware of the situation. With the help of Rosie's church friends, appropriate arrangements were made and the matter was settled. Final services were held over the weekend and Julie's boss had given her one day off. Julie was angered by his insensitivity. This day, June eighth, was her first day back to work, and she was emotionally struggling. She was longing for Toby's scheduled return in two days. In spite of it all, her glowing personality masked her true feelings.

The ladies' boss, Mr. Willard Piddledinger, was expected to pick up the extensive supply order

Julie had completed several days ago. He was also tasking the other women to complete several letters of requisition and other business correspondence.

Julie, uncharacteristically, arrived ten minutes late. Her working friends were already there to greet her. Nettie Schlosser, who had become a close confidant, was offering her condolences when Mr. Piddledinger walked in. He strode by Julie and Nettie without saying a word and began verbally deriding Beatrice, the typist.

"I brought you this letter last week for corrections, and you still haven't gotten it corrected. Look at this word here, you've spelled it two different ways. How do you expect me to send out correspondence when it makes me look illiterate?"

Beatrice looked at the work he was pointing to, and found it was the word *right.* The other word referred to was *write.*

Beatrice, near tears explained, "Sir the words are pronounced the same, but they have different meanings. I believe I have spelled them correctly, because the first is used to indicate correctness, or the opposite of left, and the other means to communicate on paper, and sir, there is even another spelling that is *wright,* meaning to position something correctly. After you asked me to correct the word, I researched it, and I am sure your letter is now correct."

Piddledinger paused, and with no humility said, "Well then, I suppose you are correct; however, I so often have to correct your errors that I have become quite alert to their frequent occurrence."

He quickly turned to face Julie, who was looking at him with disgust after rolling her eyes out loud. With his hand on his hip he said, "Do you finally have that major purchase order ready for my approval?"

Her cheeriness nearly approached sarcasm when she chirped back, "Yes sir, it has been ready for eight days now."

"Oh really! Miss Carlson, it is not your responsibility to measure my time table, so let's have the report now."

Julie handed him a long list of inventoried service items, and a purchase order to restock used and depleted items. The order included a thousand pieces of crockery and glass, three hundred table cloths, seven hundred pieces of silverware, seventy-eight mattresses, two hundred sheets and blankets, and a footnote recommending the hiring of nine additional cooks and thirty-six waiters.

She watched the dreadful little man, as he exploded in faux indignity. "How in the world am I supposed to price all of these items and get this order out in two days?"

Julie, once again lost her patience. Unable to indulge what she believed was repetitious, ignorant, arrogance, calmly pointed out, "If you look on the last page, they are all conveniently priced and listed in alphabetical order."

Humiliated again, Piddledinger burst into a tyrannical rage. "This job has to be the worst this organization has to offer. I have to put up with insubordinate women who have no appreciation of the real work that I attend to. I don't know how management brain washed me into accepting such a position."

As he turned to leave, Julie again cheerily responded, "Mr. Piddledinger, we apologize for our gender, but because of it, the NP can hire us for less. I'm truly sorry that you are unhappy in your current profession. Perhaps you can make a change. It will be interesting to see what you become when you grow up."

Julie heard a stifled laugh from Nettie as Piddledinger stomped out of the office.

As soon as it was safe to speak, Nettie said, "Julie, you scare me. I don't know how you do it. You are the most likeable, well mannered, proper woman I know, yet you have the kick of a mule. If any one of us spoke up as you did, we would surely be fired."

"No you wouldn't Nettie. Littledinger needs every one of you."

As Julie changed the name, the other ladies burst into laughter, causing Nettie to admonish, "And that's another thing. If you keep referring to him as Littledinger, one of us is going to slip someday and call him that in his presence."

Again the room was filled with laughter.

Julie said, "I'm sorry friends, I just can't develop any respect for him. You know that he is the NP President's nephew. He didn't get the job because of his talent. He said they brainwashed him into the job. That's a joke. You could brainwash him using a thimble for a bucket."

With that pronouncement, the crew was a carnival of laughter. By now Julie had lost her state of depression and began venting feelings she had suppressed for months.

"You are all laughing, but I know everyone was thinking these thoughts. I just said it. That man has delusions of adequacy. He's an example of a self-made man who loves his creator, and he expects a granite monument just for being toilet trained."

The room was silent now, its occupants awed by Julie's rare display of anger. She continued, "I know sometimes I step out of bounds, beyond the line of what a proper woman is supposed to be. I don't care what Littledinger thinks; I am who I am, and his approval isn't needed. You know why he doesn't pick on me? It's because I intimidate him with confidence. You ladies should do the same."

Wilma spoke up, "Julie, you are in a different position. You have numerous talents. I need this job, and there are women all over town that would like to get out of doing laundry and scrubbing toilets for a few dollars a month. Here I make a dollar thirty-four cents a day. They would jump on my job with both feet."

"Wilma, you imprison yourself with your own thoughts. I was once kidnapped and enslaved into laundry work and my captors had even worse plans for me; but I broke away. Those women you refer to cannot write like you. They cannot operate one of those new typing machines, nor do the other jobs you routinely accomplish. When you are being spit on by people like Littledinger, you have to spit back or they will dominate you. That's what it's all about, control. It's his only real accomplishment. Without his uncle, he would go no further than an unaddressed envelope. Yes, I know that you will think I am insensitive. Ladies, truth knows no insensitivity."

Julie walked back to her desk, slammed down her tablet and said, "Now, let's all get back to work, and at exactly eleven forty-eight, I am going to take us all to lunch."

Nine

On the fifth day of counting on Monday, June seventh, all three boys found themselves challenged with counting a large number of sheep. Timmy had worked out their partnership allowing them all to be paid fairly for their efforts. Because he was the original employee and therefore the boss, he divided the ten cent an hour earnings so that he received four cents and the other two each received three cents per hour. On this day they earned their pay, finishing late in the afternoon. As agreed, they would turn in their official count the next morning. But there was a problem. Each one had a different total number of sheep. They differed by four sheep. Eddy insisted on precise accuracy and recommended each of them count independently to assure the count was correct. But today it wasn't.

After arguing the count for several minutes they resolved to separate the animals into smaller pens and recount them. They were capable of moving the sheep, but it would soon be dark and if they weren't home before then, their parents would be searching for them.

Timmy took charge of the situation. "Look, we can't tell Eddy that we have different counts. And we can't make up a number that's just close. We have to be right. Anything else will cause Eddy to lose confidence in us, and we'll be back to spending the day fishing for suckers in the river. Let's come back early in the morning, before anyone else is here and do our recount."

They all agreed. Timmy provided the final instructions. "The sun starts pushing back the dark around four in the morning. As soon as there is any light at all, we will meet at the edge of the river behind old lady Grayson's pasture. We should be able to finish in a little more than two hours and can give Eddy the count by seven and no one will know the difference."

It was a short night, but at daybreak, on Tuesday, they all were present near the edge of the pasture even though they could barely see where they were walking. The air was brisk and the early morning dew soaked their pants halfway to their knees.

Timmy was still giving directions. "Let's cut across Grayson's pasture and take the short cut through the trees so we end up at the back side of the corrals. We don't want anyone to see us out here at this time of the morning or they will think we are up to no good."

As Timmy, Chubby and Joe attempted to quietly tramp through the high grass, they were anything but silent. Chubby was known for his big feet and clumsy gait. Chubby tripped over a stick and fell like a wounded moose into the edge of a wild rose bush.

Joe said, "For God's sake Chubby, pick up your feet."

Chubby returned to his feet a little scratched and scolded Joe by saying, "You don't have to cuss. That wasn't necessary."

Joe countered, "I wasn't cussing."

"Yes you were, you said God. My mom says you shouldn't say God unless you are praying."

"Well then I was praying to God that you would learn to pick up your feet."

As they walked, Timmy urged them to be quieter, but the argument between Chubby and Joe continued.

Chubby said, "No, that's cussing. Good people don't cuss."

Joe disagreed. "Everyone cusses once in a while. I even heard my teacher cuss."

"No, not Mr. Harrison. I don't believe it."

"Yes, last winter, Nancy Holloway went to him and asked to go to the outhouse. He told her to wait until Tilly Johnstone returned, but before she could say anything, she threw up all over Mr. Harrison's desk. He said, 'Damn Girl, step back.' Then the whole class started laughing, and he hollered, 'OK class, every one of you put your heads down on your desk, and I don't want to hear a damn peep out of you until I get this cleaned up.' He was really mad, and swore twice."

Chubby said, "Eddy wouldn't like it if he heard us cussing. He doesn't cuss."

Joe returned, "Oh yes he does. I heard him one time. Remember this spring when it rained for three days and everything was sloppy muddy? I was over by the corrals watching Eddy and that old guy move some of the watering troughs up to the higher spots so the cattle wouldn't have to stand in the muck. Eddy was tugging on one end of a trough when two bulls were pushing each other around near him. One of the bulls ran into Eddy, knocked over the trough and sent Eddy sprawling face first into the muddy cow slop. It was so deep he had to do a push up to get his face out of the cow poop. With his arms in the goop up to his elbows he looked up and you could barely see his eyes through the crap running down his face. He sure cussed then. He said –"

"Hold it," Timmy interrupted. "We don't want to know what he said."

"Well I'm not sure I could tell you anyway because some of it I never heard before, and I don't even know what it means. I thought about asking my Dad about it but figured he would whip my butt for even repeating some of the words, so I just forgot about it until now."

Timmy, relatively silent until now sadly said, "I wish I had a Dad. I wish I had a dad for a lot of things, but I wish I had a dad to tell me about cussing."

Chubby, still stumbling forward through the grass asked, "Why would you wish for that?"

"Because you have to know how to cuss to do it right. You can't pretend to be mad and just go around cussing if you don't know what to say. You have to practice so it comes naturally. Anyone who cusses without knowing his stuff really sounds dumb."

Joe chimed back in, "For sure. Girls really sound stupid when they try to cuss."

Chubby thought, "Do girls cuss?"

Joe continued, "Sure they do. But I think they only cuss when they're just with other girls."

Timmy snickered, "I think I would cuss too if I had to be only with girls."

After a period of silence, Timmy closed the discussion, "I think maybe I'll ask Eddy if he will teach me how to cuss. It's just something a guy should know."

They were only a hundred yards from their destination at the far end of the corrals, but had not yet emerged from the tall grass and brush when Timmy, in the lead, slapped Chubby's side and said, "Git down!" They all squatted in the bushes and looked toward the corrals. Only a few feet in front of them were two men, busy working over something on the ground. The boys crawled into the tall grass, then parted it to see better. The men were in a small clearing, bending over two dead cows. Both were cutting on separate animals, but didn't appear to be skinning them. They were talking softly but a few words were understandable.

What they heard was, "Well leave them here.... throw them off track.... quit looking at the books." Additional words were mumbled, but none of it made sense to the boys.

Then one of the men bent over the cow's right flank and began removing the hide containing the brand. Chubby had his head near the ground with pollen from the grass rising up into his face. He felt it coming, his eyes watered, his nose tickled he tried holding his breath, yet couldn't stifle the onrush. He sneezed like a snorting buffalo. Both men stood up and cussed, while one said "What was that?"

Timmy and Chubby were well hidden in the tall grass, but Joe was on the outside near the path to the corrals. When they saw him, one of the men said, "It's a damn kid" and started in the boys' direction. Joe was a quick thinker, and an even faster runner. When the men advanced toward him, he sprang into an all-out run in the opposite direction of his two friends. The second man was slower, but he too joined in pursuit. He ran very close to Chubby but didn't notice him while he was concentrating on catching Joe. The young sprinter, Joe, was increasing his distance, but the cursing runner behind him was also fleet. Joe tried dodging in different directions and circled around toward the river, but the man, with longer legs was cutting corners and not falling behind. Only once Joe looked behind. He was terrified to see a tall lean adult running after him wielding a long skinning knife, with blood still dripping from handle to point. Finally, as he cut through a thick stand of willows, the knife man tripped over a root and crashed onto the river sand. Joe kept running until he was sure he separated himself from danger. He tiptoed over rocks along the river edge to avoid leaving any tracks. He was sure he narrowly escaped death, but his quick action drew the men away from Timmy and Chubby, allowing their escape back into the thicker brush.

Joe crept safely back into the river brush and his two friends lay low in the weeds bordering the corrals. If Timmy or Chubby dared to look out toward the running cow killers, they risked being exposed. Both attempted to stifle their heavy breathing and listened. Joe, being very familiar with the river front, secreted himself in a position where he could observe his adversaries on their return. He got a good look at the knife wielding one, and adding to his fright, Joe noticed the second stockier man had unholstered his long-barreled revolver.

The man who chased Joe the furthest returned to the kill site out of breath and angry. Both of the hiding boys could hear the conversation.

He said to the other, "I don't know how much that kid saw, but he won't be able to identify us. He may have run to tell somebody, so let's get the hell out of here. We were supposed to skin these cattle and partly cut them up, but this is good enough. Somebody will find this and get the cart rolling. Just don't tell Bossman we didn't finish."

They hastily strode out of sight, and the sound of galloping horses running toward Fort Keogh told the boys the men we gone.

Timmy and Chubby ran back to where they were sure Joe had retreated. They found him lurking near their "secret" treehouse next to the Tongue River. He was hesitant to reveal himself until he was sure they were alone.

Joe asked in a shaky voice, "What was all that about? Who were those guys?"

Timmy proposed, "I think they stole those cows and were going to butcher them there."

Joe wasn't sure. "Then why did they run off and leave them."

Again Timmy answered, "Because they saw you and thought you would be able to get them into trouble by telling someone. We heard them say so. I don't know who they were, but they'd kill us all if they found out we saw anything and could talk about it."

Chubby finally spoke, "Then we better keep our mouths shut, because a whole bunch of people know we are working at the stockyards."

Timmy frowned, "Don't you think we should tell Eddy?"

"How are we gonna explain why we were out here at five in the morning, messing around at the corrals?", said Joe, "I think we should keep quiet and see what happens. We don't even know where the cows came from and we sure don't know who those guys are."

Timmy thought it over and agreed. "OK, what we need to do is go back there and get our count right. We can give it to Eddy, and skedaddle back home before somebody finds the cows. Then when we come back tomorrow, we can figure out if what we saw is important."

They all agreed, and returned to the stockyard through the front side, avoiding the dead cows. They hurried through the count, matched their numbers and left Timmy to submit their count to Eddy.

Later, when Eddy arrived, he was surprised to find Timmy waiting for him. He gave Eddy what he purported to be the previous day's sheep count and turned to leave. Eddy recognized that he was not his usual talkative self and asked, "Hey, you're here early this morning and seem to be in a hurry. Is everything OK? How's your mom?"

"She's OK. I got up early this morning and haven't seen her yet today. I need to get back home to get something to eat before she goes to work."

"That's fine Timmy. We probably won't have any stock to count until tomorrow afternoon. I'll let you know if you'll stop by around lunch time."

Eddy organized his men getting the sheep loaded back into their cattle cars to be transported further east. The job had just been completed when a United States Marshal found Eddy at the feed shed.

"You Eddy Kingston?", the Marshal asked.

"Yup, what can I do for ya?"

"I understand you are in charge of this entire stockyards. Is that right?"

Eddy nodded in agreement, and looked at the Marshal for more information.

"I got a report this morning that a couple of men from the stockyards were butchering two cows that they had stolen from the pens."

"I don't think so Marshal. The only thing we have had in the pens since yesterday afternoon is sheep. My men don't show up here until seven in the morning unless we have to get a load out on an early train."

"Well Mr. Kingston, I figure that anyone stealing a couple of cows might come to work a little early to avoid being caught. I'd like to have a look around."

"That's fine Marshal. I'll go with you. The pens reach clear back to those trees just up from the river."

Eddy walked with the lawman who seemed to know exactly where he was going. They proceeded to the rear of the pen complex, near where the boys had been earlier that morning. It was not long before they came upon two freshly killed beef cattle.

Eddy was flabbergasted, and the Marshal was not impressed with Eddy's reaction.

"These cows did not come from these pens!", Eddy exclaimed. "Who the heck would kill a couple of cows and leave them right here, if they stole them from the pens?"

"That's what I intend to find out", offered the Marshal. He did a quick search of the scene, but discovered very little.

Eddy recognized the area that should have displayed a brand on the largest animal had been removed. He pointed it out to the Marshal. The response was, "That's to be expected. It's often the first cuts made. You know it's pretty hard to sell a branded stolen hide."

Eddy, sensing where this was going, began working to regain control. He grabbed the leg of the smallest cow and said to the Marshal, "Help me roll this one over and we'll look for a brand in the same area as it seemed to be cut from the big one. They might be from the same ranch."

Both struggled with the stiffening carcass until they exposed it's second side. To Eddy's satisfaction, the animal carried a clean brand. The symbols =J, or "Double Bar J" were clearly showing through the hair.

Eddy said, "I think I know that brand, and I think it is a local mark. I'll check around to see who might own these cows."

The Marshal replied, "You best leave that to me. Now I'd like to start with a list of your employees. The information left by the witness showed he was pretty sure the men who killed these cows were either you or a couple of your men."

Suddenly, Eddy recognized the setup. He needed help to change the direction of these implications. He knew his men would have nothing to do with these killings, but he had no idea who would want him blamed for the NP's cattle losses. Toby's message said that "Confidentially" he resolved the issue, but it sure didn't look like it from the back of his corrals this morning. Eddy wisely interpreted Toby's admonition to not discuss the matter; probably because he was not completely finished with his inquiry. That meant he couldn't tell the Marshal the latest information, because not even he was aware of any details. He decided to cooperate with the Marshal until he could contact Toby, who hopefully could sort this out.

Eddy walked the Marshal back to his office. The scene was tense, with few words spoken. Eddy wrote out a list of his employees, and handed it to the Marshal, who inquired, "Is this all of them?"

Eddy responded, "That's everybody except three boys that do the stock counting."

"Where are they?"

"I don't know, they're just kids. They only show up when I need them."

"Well you need them now because I want to talk to everyone who's had anything to do with the cattle going through this place. What are their names?"

"I only know their first names, Timmy, Chubby, and Joe. I told you, they are just kids."

"When can you have them here?"

"I don't know. They don't always drop by every day. Maybe I can have them here by tomorrow afternoon."

The Marshal thought for a moment and said, "OK, I'll be here early in the afternoon unless something else keeps me, but I must warn you that I have been briefed on the stock losses by the railroad, and cattle theft is taken very seriously in these parts of the Territory."

Eddy snorted, "As if I didn't know."

Without speaking, the Marshal strode off to his waiting mount.

Ten

Eddy's first effort was to locate Toby. He rushed to the depot and sent a telegram to Spokane, only to receive a reply that Toby departed early this morning. He wouldn't have a scheduled stop until Billings, which would be late at night, somewhere around midnight, and if he couldn't be reached there, it would be Bismarck before he could get a telegram to him through the Bismarck depot. He could attempt to get the train to stop at Miles City, but it was not scheduled to do so. At three in the morning an unscheduled stop would cause the delay of several other trains in the vicinity. Desperate for a solution he entered the managerial offices to discuss the problem with the Depot Master. However by the time he gained an audience with the man in charge, the rumor had already been spread about the livestock shortages being the fault of Eddy and his crew. The Depot Master declined to cooperate in interrupting the passenger service. Eddy needed some improved luck. He decided the only sure way to reach Toby was to cause the Bismarck Train Station to locate Toby and deliver a telegram. Toby penned the message and instructed the telegrapher to send it immediately.

The message was: URGENT, IMMEDIATLY DELIVER TO TOBIAS HAWTHORN ABOARD EASTBOUND NP PASSENGER SERVICE # 233 THIS DATE. US MARSHAL AT MILES INVESTIGATING ACCUSATION OUR STATION RESPONSIBLE FOR STOCK LOSSES. BUTCHERED COWS FOUND NEAR CORRALS THIS MORNING. BELIEVE COWS ARE FROM LOCAL AREA, NOT NP. MARSHAL CONCENTRATING ON US. YOUR ASSISTANCE NEEDED IMMEDIATELY TO EXPOSE TRUTH. MARSHAL RETURNING TOMORROW AFTERNOON.

The man receiving the message looked at Eddy inquisitively, but said nothing. Because it was NP business, Eddy departed without being charged.

Eddy had many connections throughout the Territory, but this problem was too personal to share with anyone but the closest of friends. He now spurred his horse toward the sawmill at the edge of town. His longtime friend Jim Young Bear was there, and Jim was among the best trackers in the Territory. He would ask Jim to use his unmatched tracking abilities.

Eddy found Jim, working at the sawmill on the green chain. It took only seconds for him to explain why he needed Jim to trace a trail to the original location of the two dead cows at the north end of the stockyards. Jim checked out of the sawmill six minutes later.

The ride to the dead animals was quick. Although they had only been killed in the early hours of the day, they were already beginning to decay.

Eddy wanted to salvage the meat, but he didn't dare disturb the scene, knowing the Marshal would object with additional accusations.

Jim examined the kill site, said the animals were led to the location by two men on foot, wearing boots, and struck in the head with a blunt object, probably stunning them until their throats were cut. Young Bear mounted his pony and told Eddy, "I'll be back when I know something."

Eddy was confident that for Jim, the task of following the trail of two cows and two horses through river bottom country should be as easy as a kid following railroad tracks. He returned to his stockyard office to restore calm, before another uprising.

Eddy was a high energy person, and intolerant when it came to theft. By afternoon he was oozing with anger at the idea he was being accused of stealing from his company, and the stockmen whom he worked with. He vowed that someone would pay dearly for this clear setup. Who would want to frame him? Surely Toby would have some answers, but waiting was maddening.

When Timmy wandered in, it was mid-afternoon, a regular time for his check in. Eddy immediately noticed that his demeanor was quiet and subdued. He stayed out of everyone's way, asked no questions and delivered none of his usual daily trivia. Eddy, reluctant to inform him of the recent incidents, chose to only state the need for his command attendance at tomorrow's meeting. Eddy drew him aside, but the conversation was awkward.

"Timmy come over here a second, I have to explain something. There's been a misunderstanding about our handling of the livestock. A U.S. Marshal is coming here tomorrow afternoon to talk to us about it, and he wants to speak to you and your two friends, Chubby and Joe."

Timmy's eyes widened. He looked up at Eddy and said, "Are we in trouble for our counting?"

Eddy affectionately patted him on the back and rubbed his fingers through the kid's tousled hair, saying, "No Timmy, you have done nothing wrong. And neither has any of the rest of us. As I said, it is a misunderstanding, and that's why we are meeting about it. A couple of cows have died and we need to explain that we had nothing to do with it. Now Timmy be sure you are here tomorrow by one in the afternoon, and have you friends with you."

Timmy said, "Yes Sir", and exploded in a full run toward the river.

Eddy mused, "I wonder what's wrong with him. He never even asked any questions."

* * * * * * *

Timmy ran the quarter mile to meet Joe and Chubby who were waiting at the treehouse. As he halted panting, Joe asked, "What's wrong with you? You look like a bear's been chasing you?"

"Guys, it's a lot worse than that", Timmy gasped. "We are going to be talked to by a US Marshal tomorrow afternoon, and we all have to be there." The others sat in silence while Timmy continued. "Eddy said it's about a couple of cows that died and we need to prove we didn't have anything to do with it."

Chubby groaned, "Oh no! But we did."

Joe differed, "No we didn't. We didn't have anything to with killing those cows!"

Timmy said, "No, but we saw what happened, so now we have to tell why we were there, and explain what we saw."

Joe thought out loud, "Oh crap. Now Eddy's gonna be mad at us because we didn't come tell him right away. How we gonna explain that?"

Chubby said, "We don't have to tell them we can't count sheep. All we have to say is that we stumbled onto these guys at the edge of the woods."

Joe's response was, "Oh sure. We all three were just out for a walk at four-thirty in the morning, wet to our butts in dew, practicing silent tepee creeping when we innocently came upon two cattle rustlers with blood dripping from their knives; and that we were all so dumb we didn't think it was important to tell somebody. No guys, that ain't gonna work. We'll all get locked up for lying."

Chubby, stifling a throat choking sob said, "We haven't lied yet. But I'm afraid of those guys. What if they would have caught us?"

Joe said, "If they would have caught me, my guts would have been spread out there mixed in with the cow's blood. And Chubby, if they would have seen your sneezing face, you'd be lying in the grass with the ravens picking out your eyes."

"Yaagh!", Chubby screamed, slapping his hands over his eyes and burying his face in his lap. "Joe don't talk like that! I won't sleep for the rest of the summer. Maybe we should arm ourselves."

Joe asked, "With what?"

Timmy offered, "I have a slingshot."

Chubby said, "My mom won't let me carry my fishing knife, but I have a baseball bat."

Joe scoffed, "Oh great! How you gonna go round carrying a baseball bat? I can just see you going to church with your Ma, carrying a baseball bat. 'Good morning Reverend. You wanna hit a few fly balls?' No, if we don't tell Eddy something, we'll have no protection at all. He'll figure out how to keep these guys from coming after us."

Timmy, with fear still in his eyes, said, "My mom always tells me that when you are in trouble, the most important thing you can do is be honorable and tell the truth. She says that people will judge you more by your honesty than your mistakes."

Joe said, "Well maybe, but boy this is gonna hurt."

Chubby added, "Hurt ain't the word. If those guys find out we saw them and are ratting them out, they are gonna kill us."

Timmy said, "We already discussed that, but would you rather die a liar or a brave stupid, kid? We got no choice but to stick together and explain that we ran because we were scared, and that we didn't say anything until we thought it was safe to do so."

Chubby brightened up and said, "Yah, that doesn't sound so bad. Who's gonna do the talking?"

They all looked at each other, followed by a moment of silence. Joe broke the mood with, "Timmy, you got us all into this, and Eddy likes you the best, so you need to be the hero speaker. If you're gonna tell the truth, then there is only one story to tell, and we will all be in agreement. That way if they separate us and ask questions, we will all have the same answers. You guys saw more than I did, because I took off running, thinking you would be safe if they followed me. I knew I could outrun them and I did. I didn't look back until I couldn't hear the guy crashing after me."

Chubby nodded, and Timmy agreed. "Ok, I'll tell the truth, and you guys back me up if they start giving me trouble. We'll just have to look out for each other later, and not worry about those guys coming back after us. The more I think about it, those guys don't know there were three of us, and they don't know where anyone lives. Maybe we're making the problem more than it is. Eddy is our friend and I think he needs help. So let's do it."

Eleven

Wednesday morning was a long time arriving for Eddy. He spent most of the night awake, searching for reasons, asking himself repeatedly why all this was happening. The thought he favored was that Toby had somehow allowed the cattle thieves to know he was investigating, and the activity around his corrals was meant as a diversion.

He was beside himself, because he had not seen or heard from Jim since yesterday afternoon. He had no idea if Toby had been contacted, or if he would even get some explanation from Toby through the telegraph office. Eddy knew he was being set up, and at this point was unable to control the outcome.

Eddy was at the stockyards early. He walked down to the area where the two carcasses lie and found that the coyotes had already taken their fill. Magpies and ravens were now the current competitors for the remains. He was anxious to remove the rotting animals before they developed an odor, causing more criticism of the stockyards.

It was still early, but he provided an explanation to his employees and told them what to expect from the Marshal. After that, all he could do was wait.

The morning shipping report was brought in from the Depot. This afternoon, a train carrying one thousand hogs would arrive from the west, needing water, feed and their mandatory five-hour rest. Eddy wondered what else could happen. Of all the animals cared for at the stockyards, he disliked hogs the most. They were often wild, unruly and required the most care. All of this, while he was being accused of being a thief. This was going to be a day to remember.

At twelve-thirty, a buggy stopped at the side of the road near the feed shed. The driver was an old buffalo hunter Eddy knew, but he didn't immediately recognize the passenger. As the buggy pulled away, a familiar voice came from the passenger still dressed in "city" clothes. "Eddy, what the heck are you in to now?" Toby had arrived.

In the short few minutes before the Marshal arrived, Toby explained the miracles of the NP mail system which got him back to Miles City. Outgoing mail is placed in a tough canvas bag and hung on a pole outside the depots. Postal workers in the mail cars snag the bags with a long hook as the train rumbles past. The mail car is a traveling post office handling baggage and mail. Workers sort and place the mail into pigeon holes for delivery, eventually to be bagged and tossed out at other depots along the line, or transferred to trains traveling in the opposite direction.

Eddy's telegram was sent to Bismarck, was put aboard a west bound train, then offloaded at Glendive, Montana Territory, transferred to Toby's passenger train in the dark hours of the morning as it passed through Glendive, and was delivered to him just before reaching Sidney, near the North Dakota Territory border. Toby was told he could debark and catch the next westbound freight train, ride in the caboose, and reach Miles City by noon. Toby was now standing in front of Eddy at the Miles City stockyards, but he was not happy.

In spite of his anger, Toby was still his calm, contemplative self. His anger was not directed at Eddy. He fully appreciated Eddy's predicament. He was furious that these scoundrels, some of which he had identified, could scheme to shift the blame for their crimes onto Eddy and his crew. He now realized that the conversation he witnessed between Angela Vincent-Coulter and her brother, Scar-neck, (Frank Vincent), had resulted in this diversionary incident. Now instead of arriving in St. Paul to a waiting Julie, he was a thousand miles away with more unanswered questions, and more crooks in the operation.

Before he could explain his findings to Eddy, the "counting trio" began to trickle in. Timmy, Chubby and Joe, all three, looked as if they had just been whipped by the school principal. They sat timidly at the edge of the feed shed; a long wooden structure with a tin roof, and an open wall to the northeast. It was filled three-quarters full with alfalfa hay and barrels of ground grain. It was also a shady place for the men to rest and contained various seats, from overturned buckets to cut tree stumps. All now sat under the tin, as if waiting for the concert master to take the stage at a famous opera. Everyone was accounted for, except Jim Young Bear.

The Marshal arrived promptly at one-thirty, accompanied by a deputy. Toby could not help but notice that the deputy carried not one, but two pairs of handcuffs in his gun belt. Toby remained silent, and unnoticed as the "concert master" took the stage.

The Marshal began by explaining the nature of his investigation, with strong implications that he had a good understanding of what and why the incident in question occurred. It was, in his mind, because certain employees at the stockyard were thieves. According to his instructions, all personnel were to wait under the shed until he and his deputy could privately question them individually.

At this point Toby stood up and spoke loudly, "Marshal, I believe I can provide information that will make all that unnecessary."

The Marshal asked bluntly, "And who are you?"

"My name is Tobias Hawthorn. I'm on the NP management staff out of St. Paul. I'm just returning from Spokane, Washington, after doing an investigation concerning the stock shortages we have been experiencing."

"So what does Spokane have to do with what's going on here?"

"The Spokane investigation discloses the shortages were bookkeeping manipulations creating phantom, non-existent animals on which crooked cattle brokers collected."

"Well Mr. Hawthorn, I guess you haven't seen the two dead cows at the lower end of the stockyards. I'm here to find out who killed them. They sure ain't, as you say phantom cows." The Marshal ended his sentence with an uplift in tone that resonated like a mocking sneer.

Eddy held his breath. He knew that Toby's remarkable wit and education was unmatched when it came to verbally addressing a person or problem. Toby confided that as a home-schooled child, he was once punished by his mother after uttering a word of profanity. He was thereafter required each week, to memorize from the dictionary, one hundred words and their meaning. Toby learned to enjoy the task and continued until his mind now seemed to be part dictionary.

Now Toby's temperature was rising. A furrow in his forehead deepened, and his eyes blazed a warning. "Marshal, I see no reason for you to objurgate these people by a lengthy questioning when, if you will allow me the time, I can provide the motive for this incident. If you continue to traduce their existence with pestiferous calumny, your public obloquy will discredit both you and your office."

The Marshal looked at Toby with an expression that revealed his mental interpretation, which was "What did you just say?"

Eddy's stomach tightened. Toby's first verbal shot was to throw the Marshal off his plan, and Eddy knew that more was coming. He also noticed the accompanying deputy carried two sets of hand cuffs, clearly anticipating the need. He feared Toby had blistered the Marshal's obvious ego to the point he would make an infamous Territorial lawman's move, and arrest both of them on some ridiculous charge; perhaps for "felonious mopery." He and Toby had been to jail together in the past, and Eddy did not want a repeat performance.

Just as the Marshal and Toby were about to get into an intemperate argument, two riders appeared at the end of the feed shed, one being Jim Young Bear, and the other an aged, weathered cowboy. All conversation stopped as the two dismounted and walked into the gathering.

The Marshal spoke first; directly to Jim. "Are you here to contribute something to this discussion? Otherwise you are interrupting a legal procedure."

Jim, a person of few words, gestured toward the old Cowboy, saying only, "He has something to tell you."

The old gent began his story without being asked. "I'm Len Brightman. I own the Double-Bar-Jay ranch, just over the hill there, butted up against the Fort's land. I was out fixin' fence yesterday afternoon when I saw this here Indian feller looking at somethin' in the way north pasture. I rode on down to see him, and he showed me where the fence had been cut and put back together. He said he tracked the path of a couple of cows and whoever probably cut the fence ta take the cows. He came back this sunrise and helped me count my cows. The count came up two short. Now, I got permission from the Fort to rent that grass and I figgered maybe some of those military guys had something to do with takin' the cows. But this Indian feller took me over there where the cows are dead, and I sees that they're mine because the brand is still on one of them. Now I ain't got no idea why they took two of my best beef, drove them over here, kilt 'um and left 'um there to rot. I was hope'n you fellers might have some answers, cause I sure want to find who done it."

The Marshal then revealed an important bit of information. "Well I have an anonymous letter that says two men at this yard are responsible."

Toby was instantly furious, learning the allegation came from an anonymous letter, and jumped up to interrupt, but Timmy interceded by shouting, "That ain't so!"

The audience was shocked to see the young boy so excited and paused to let him speak.

Timmy burst forth with his burdensome message. "Chubby and Joe were with me when we saw the two guys that did it, and they weren't from here."

With those few words, he had everyone's attention, and he needed no prompting to continue.

"We came up here real early in the morning to recount the sheep because the numbers were messed up. We came the back way in the tall grass so that we wouldn't be seen redoing something we should have got right in the first place. We got right up to the guys before we saw them, and they didn't know we were there until Chubby sneezed. They only saw Joe, and chased him with a knife and the other guy drew his gun. But Joe outran them, while we snuck further into the tall grass."

When Timmy, almost in a hysterical state paused, the Marshal quickly injected a question, "Did you clearly see them, and did they say anything?"

Timmy continued, "We sure did. After Joe got away, they came back and said they needed to get away because maybe he would tell someone, and then the one who had the knife said what they did was good enough to 'throw them off' and that they shouldn't tell the Bossman that they didn't finish."

The Marshal tried one more time to gain control. "Timmy, you work here at times is that correct?" Timmy nodded his head and the Marshal continued. "Now is this exactly what you saw or have you added some from your imagination."

This time, Eddy jumped to his feet, but again the trio was not to be put down. First to respond was Joe. "Mr. Marshal, it's not in any way my imagination that the cowboy chasing me with a blood dripping knife was intending to catch and kill me. I didn't imagine what all three of us heard. The guy, as he was cutting on the cow, said, 'this will throw them off' and that 'they will quit looking at the books.' And I got a good look at the one who almost caught me. He was tall and kind of skinny, dressed like a cowboy and had a cloth thing around his neck, that dropped down after he was running. When I saw him close, I could see a big scar on his neck."

With the words "scar on his neck", Eddy threw his hat on the ground and cursed, saying, "That rotten, no good - *(much too profane to print.)*

Joe whispered to Chubby, "See I told you he could cuss."

The Marshal seemed to have run out of words and Toby assumed the lead. "Boys, Eddy and I are familiar with the man we call Scar-neck, (which was said more for the benefit of the Marshal) but can you describe the other man?"

The composite answer received was that he was maybe fifty years old, sort of husky and a slow runner. He had grey hair sticking out from under a tan hat. He didn't look soft, but more like a muscled working man. The description was not complete, but for Toby and Eddy, it eliminated Bossmiller.

With the thought of eliminating the "Big B" Toby was struck with an idea.

"Timmy, what was it again that the man said about not telling something?"

The quick reply was, "He said 'Don't tell Bossman we didn't finish.'"

"Did he say *the* Bossman, or just Bossman?"

Chubby spoke for the first time. "I think he said just Bossman because I thought he was saying a guy's name."

Eddy looked at Toby and breathed, "It all makes sense now doesn't it."

Toby walked up close to the Marshal and said, "Marshal, I think we can let these people go, and the rest of this matter can be put to rest with my complete disclosure. The railroad can follow up from here. When it is resolved, we will assist in prosecuting the cattle theft."

Before Eddy joined with Toby for his briefing to the Marshal, he took the boys aside and thanked them for their bravery. He promised to explain everything in the next few days, but cautioned them to continue keeping the information to themselves. Without adding to their fright, he mentioned that "Big B", Scar-neck and the other fellow, whoever he was, were still on the loose and it wouldn't be good if any information got back to them. Then he said, "By the way, we have about a thousand hogs arriving in less than an hour. Get out your counting pencils."

Later that evening as Eddy and Toby were privately discussing the attempted framing of Eddy, they came to several conclusions. The first was that after Scar-neck met with his sister, he must have caught the first train back to the east; the one Toby was planning to take. After he saw the meeting of Angela and Scar-neck, he delayed his return to discuss the events with the Spokane Superintendent. That allowed Scar-neck to get an entire day ahead of him. Somewhere in route Scar-neck met Bossmiller and was joined by the other still unknown person. Both Eddy and Toby agreed that Bossmiller must be whom they referred to as Bossman. The question now was, "Who is the third man? Could he be the person on the invoices named Carter? Who could be so destitute for a friend, that he would partner with such bad men?"

Eddy and Toby reviewed the most recent livestock tally sheets, comparing the Billings and Miles City numbers. They were the same, indicating that any shortages had to occur at Spokane, whether they were on paper or actual vanishing cattle. Eddy commented that it was much easier to erase and change a number on paper than it was to secretly hustle away a group of rambunctious steers.

Toby had more work to do, and decided he would not allow Angela to be fired until he could identify the new participant.

Toby ended the discussion by assuring Eddy that he would clear his name and cattle station from any suspicion of livestock theft. He concluded with, "Now I have to get back up to the Depot so we can stop that three in the morning passenger train, because I am getting aboard."

As they said their good byes, Eddy had the last words in typical fashion. "I know that Marshal was just trying to do his job, but when the boys were done telling their story, he was so confused he didn't know if he should wind his butt, or scratch his watch. We couldn't have cleared this up without you. OK Bub, thanks from all of us."

Twelve

Timmy returned the morning after the interrogation with the hog count, he and his partners had completed the previous afternoon. His first question to Eddy was, "Is everything OK?"

Eddy was impressed with the boy's loyalty and devotion. He sat down with him and once again praised his bravery and explained he was not angry because they failed to immediately report their dangerous encounter.

"Timmy, I notice that your mom walks by here at times on her way to work. Could you tell her I'd like to talk with her as soon as she has the chance?"

"Yes sir! I'll tell her this afternoon."

Timmy didn't ask why, and Eddy would not have told him if he did. Eddy Kingston had a plan.

When Alice Horton stepped into Eddy's office that afternoon, he glanced at his watch. She was early, and Timmy was not with her.

After a moment of awkward small talk, Eddy initiated his plan.

"Alice, I suppose Timmy has told you about the troublesome incident we had here this week."

"Yes, he did, but I'm sure a lot of detail was left out, and I have many questions."

"I'm sure you do, so here is what I propose. The boys performed very well, and I would like to reward their behavior in a special way. This coming Sunday, I would like to take them down town for ice cream....as much as they can eat. It would be an honor if you would accompany us."

"Oh my, I would be pleased to participate. Timmy loves ice cream, but it's a rare luxury, seldom seen."

Eddy, pleased with his progress, said, "One other problem is that I don't know how to contact, or get permission of Chubby's and Joe's parents. Could you do that, or direct them to me?"

Alice agreed, saying, "Sure they are my neighbors. I will explain that I will be with them. They have heard much about you, and I'm sure they will come up to meet you soon. They really appreciate the efforts you have gone to, just to keep the boys busy."

Eddy finalized the conversation with, "Perfect! I will see you all here at one, Sunday afternoon."

Alice departed, stepping as though she was wearing "Wonderland" slippers.

* * * * * * *

On Sunday, Eddy prepared for the afternoon by harnessing the company horses and dusting off the NP hack. There would be five in the carriage, and he wanted to be sure Alice was seated beside him. She arrived on time, with all three boys scampering ahead of her. Timmy, Chubby and Joe were cleaner than he had ever seen them before, and Alice was beautiful.

The boys scampered up into the carriage before Eddy could offer a hand to Alice. Eddy commented, "Gee, I'm sorry it doesn't look like you guys like ice cream. Maybe they serve caster oil at the soda fountain." They all groaned and giggled something inaudible.

The afternoon passed with two dishes of ice cream per boy, while Eddy and Alice shared individual flavors. On their return, Eddy delivered Chubby and Joe to their homes, and stopped at the residence of Alice and Timmy. Timmy would have been content staying near Eddy, but Alice encouraged him to go outdoors and play with his friends. While the boys soiled their Sunday clothes fishing at the river, Eddy lingered until twilight drinking tea and getting to know his new friend.

Thirteen

Toby arrived in St. Paul a day late, to find his loving friend waiting in the Depot. She greeted him with open arms and hugs, while tears began flowing from her eyes. Toby, only understanding part of her emotions, apologized for his late arrival, and briefly explained the delay caused by Miles City.

Julie playfully huffed, "I might have known it had something to do with Eddy."

Shaking his head, Toby said, "No, it was serious, but Eddy's a good honest man. None of it was Eddy's fault, but a halo has to only fall a few inches to become a noose. I'll tell you all about it this evening."

As they began the walk toward Aunt Rosie's house, Julie told him the details of Rosie's passing. She told him of how she had been living in the house alone for a week, but was still emotionally unable to pack up or dispose of any of Rosie's belongings. She opined that the members of Rosie's church would gladly take possession of whatever Julie was unable to use, and distribute it to the needy. Toby willingly agreed to assist in the process.

At a quiet restaurant, both shared the experiences of the past several days. Julie joked about Piddledinger, and Toby revealed the secrets of his livestock audit. Following the current events report, Toby said, "We have some very personal plans to make. In spite of all the working demands, I have not been able to concentrate on much else."

Julie's warm smile, bathed her reply in acceptance. "After Aunt Rosie's death, I spent many hours thinking through marriage plans. Toby, neither you or I have any living relatives. We have a few friends associated with our work, but not even enough to fill a chapel. I would like to set aside anything monetary I receive from Rosie, and reserve it for something more important in our future. Aside from that we haven't the means to have a public wedding. Would you be content traveling somewhere new and having a private ceremony involving just us?"

Toby was not surprised. "I have been thinking almost the same. At the present I am a little weary of train travel, but when it is done in style, it is an experience of complete luxury. We are both NP employees. I am confident I can get our Superintendent, Mr. Hanson, to provide us with complementary first-class passenger service all the way to Portland and return. We could get married in Portland, see the West Coast, and return, enjoying at least ten days of complete luxury."

"Oh Toby, that would be wonderful. How soon can we do it?"

"I prefer to go as soon as possible before something else happens to delay us. It will take me a couple of days to report all my information, but it will take the Headquarters and legal people several more to develop a plan of action. Let's leave the middle of next week. I'll explain to Mr. Hanson that we plan to get married and want to leave Wednesday the sixteenth. I will ask for two weeks' vacation, for both of us, which is only one more day than we have saved. You can lock up Aunt Rosie's house and we will deal with it when we return. I'll ask our friend Mr. Lavine, the NP Barrister, to examine the legal aspects of transferring title to the house. He can do that while we are gone. I'll see Mr. Hanson tomorrow."

Fourteen

Mr. Hanson, the Division Superintendent, was Toby's boss and good friend. He recognized Toby's abilities and used them to further his own career, while always treating Toby fairly.

This morning he sat in his well-appointed office, anticipating Toby's arrival and informational update. Toby's early arrival did not disappoint him. The briefing and written report were detailed and complete, pleasing Mr. Hanson. Toby was congratulated on his outstanding performance, and at that moment, saw his opportunity to ask the favor.

"Sir, I'd like you to be the first with whom I share this information. Julie and I have made plans to be married."

"Well congratulations Toby! I was thinking it's about time you two lovebirds tie the knot."

"Thank you. As you know, we are both without relatives, and also because of the recent death of Julie's aunt, we have decided on a private ceremony, and would like to include a short vacation with a little travel. Would it be possible for us to travel to Portland as NP employees in first class? If need be, I can make it a business trip by doing additional investigation in Spokane."

Mr. Hanson grinned, and without hesitation replied, "Absolutely! And you will do no work on this trip. I will arrange for not only free travel, but full first-class meals and Pullman sleeper accommodations. Here, let me make a note for the travel clerks. All-inclusive first-class travel with, (he looked up and smiled) two sleeping compartments westbound and one returning."

Toby blushed, and said softly, "Thank you sir, that will be wonderful."

He turned to leave the office, but couldn't resist mentioning one item of business.

"Sir, after completing my report, I had an idea that would greatly assist us in providing security and monitoring fares on our passenger lines. I understand you will be forbidding travel by lawbreakers who are using the NP to their advantage. However, identifying and separating the good from the bad is a difficult task. We currently offer a stamped pass to the frequently traveling cattle brokers, so that they may travel at a discount. Perhaps we should offer a revokable pass that includes their full name and photograph. We could establish issuing offices at a few of the major shipping points. Thereafter, the pass would be required for brokers to obtain the discount, and would eliminate many freeloaders posing as cattle brokers. It would also allow us to recognize those who we identify as undesirable."

Mr. Hanson, spoke seriously, "Toby, that is an idea that may solve several problems. Once again you have demonstrated why we value your service with the NP. Now go and tell that wonderful lady, that you both have our full blessings, and you need not meet any schedules. I'll grant extra days off for this type of occasion. When you return, we'll discuss a proper salary for a married executive."

Fifteen

For the past several months, Julie had been living with or near her Mother and Aunt. They were quite generous, rarely allowing Julie to share in expenses. As a result, she possessed a fine wardrobe and wore it well. She consulted Toby concerning their expected activities other than train travel. He suggested sightseeing in Portland, and perhaps a trip to the Pacific Ocean, which was also accessible by train. They hoped to conclude the trip with a stop in Miles City, to visit with Eddy and meet his new lady friend. Both agreed it was time for Eddy to "settle down" and they meant to provide encouragement. For the last outing, Toby suggested riding clothes, knowing that Julie loathed sidesaddles, large hoop dresses and petticoats.

Toby helped secure Aunt Rosie's house, reminding himself, although it was hard to believe, it was now Julie's house. They planned to return in approximately ten days to address the problems of inheritance.

On June sixteenth, 1886, Toby and Julie boarded the westbound express train for Portland, Oregon Territory. This was going to be a trip of a little more than seventeen hundred miles, taking more than fifty hours. It was most exciting for Julie who had never fully enjoyed the luxury of her own efforts to make the dining and Pullman cars an experience equal to fine hotels and restaurants. For the first time she would see the grandeur of the developing West. It was a first big step into adulthood, and the independence from the mundane chores of daily survival. It was a grand day, and she fully realized the implications of it all.

For three days and two nights the pair, dined as never before, drank in the views, and dreamed of their future. Toby was acquainted with many of the employees. He won the admiration and respect of all. Each strove to impress with their finest of supply and service. Toby graciously accepted the flattery, but Julie, always poised when in view, privately chided Toby for existing as a "big shot."

She commented with glee, "Now Toby, to maintain your image, you must remember this is a moving dining room. You should always order soup that matches your pants." Her comments were good natured, because she truly enjoyed being the princess of the prince.

Spring rain in Portland did not dampen their spirits. On their first day, Saturday, they chose the Chapel in which they would be married. The clergyman arranged to perform the ceremony right after church services on Sunday. They spent the afternoon completing the documentation the clergyman had required.

The Sunday congregation slowly departed. As the groups shuffled out into the City, Toby felt his body tensing, in spite of his confidence in his commitment. He and July walked to the front of the Chapel where they took a seat and waited for the minister's return. The pleasant man, clothed in a white robe approached from the back of the church, stepped in front of the timid pair and said smiling, "Did you two have something in mind?"

The event was witnessed by a few who saw Toby place his ring on Julie's finger and lingered to share in the joy.

The next three days were spent among the clear rivers, tall trees and damp air of Oregon Territory. A short train ride to the ocean, delivered the experience of fresh seafood, barking seals, and wind driven white caps spilling onto salty sand.

Sixteen

The newlyweds reluctantly appeared at the Portland Depot for departure on the evening of Wednesday June twenty-third, a full week from the beginning of their journey. Both settled into their coach seats feeling an uneasiness with the thought of re-entering the noise, confusion, and unnatural stuffiness of their city existence. More than once during their week of togetherness, memories of the Musselshell and Montana Territory were mentioned. Julie was actually looking forward to visiting Eddy Kingston in Miles City. At one point Julie asked, "Toby, how can one be homesick, when she no longer has a home to be sick about?"

Toby's reply was, "Home is not a building. It's often even more than a location. I think it's a place where your soul feels comfortable living with the memories you have absorbed and the life you have lived. Your mother left you your family's world in the land of the Musselshell. I sense that you need to revisit that world to view it through your mature eyes. We were both only fourteen when we were torn out of there."

"Toby, can we do that sometime? Do you think we could do that before this winter? The railroads could get us reasonably close?"

"Julie, if that's what you want, we'll figure out how to do it, one way or another."

The return to the East continued to be delightful and luxurious. The hours passed quickly while they sat together marveling at the beauty of America. Julie was excited with the prospect of stepping off into Miles City as Mrs. Tobias Hawthorn.

They had been traveling more than twenty-four hours when they briefly stopped in Butte, Montana Territory. Toby, customarily left the train and walked through the Depot at most places, just for the exercise, and to familiarize himself with every station. It was getting dark, but he witnessed a freight wagon and four men unloading two heavy crates into the baggage car. The activity drew his attention only because heavy freight was not usually the burden of the baggage and mail handlers. Anything over a certain weight usually went to the regular freight cars. He passed it off as being something that required rapid, or express delivery. Giving the matter no more thought, he returned to the Pullman car to prepare for the night. They would pass through Billings early in the morning and arrive in Miles City by noon.

At dawn, Julie was up and urging Toby to prepare himself for Miles City. Toby pointed out that they had just entered Billings, and it would be another four hours before arriving in their favorite cattle town. Her enthusiasm unabated, she dressed in her riding clothes, becoming a portrait of the modern 1886 horsewoman. Her clay colored, split riding skirt, new leather boots, loose sleeved white blouse topped with a blue silk scarf, and crowned with a fashionable pecan brown hat worn over her plaited golden hair defined her as a lady of distinction.

As the train lurched out of Billings, they were seated at their usual place in the dining car with waiters competing for Julie's attention. Toby sat quietly savoring his coffee and enjoying the spectacle. He was grateful to not have seen any of the villain travelers of the previous weeks. It was as if they had all fled in fright, even before they were banned from the NP line. He had not told Julie of the threat he had received from the gamblers. There was no need to introduce any type of apprehension during this most wonderful of times.

Trainmen communicated with lanterns and whistles. The lantern was the most important tool used to signal the engineer to stop, slow, reverse and warn of other trains of obstacles on the track. Brakemen and switchmen held a clear colored lantern and signaled with specific arm movements. Depot and trackside lanterns colored red meant stop, yellow was for caution or slow, and green meant all clear. The most important signal, seldom used, was the blue light. Anything blue required an emergency stop, for either track damage, or repairmen working on the ground.

Now resting in the passenger coach, Toby pointed to the Pompey's Pillar Rock out the left side windows, retelling how he and his father forded the

Yellowstone River near there during their search to find the NP railroad construction. He noted that the scene had changed little since 1881, except the river was now swollen from the spring runoff.

Just after they passed the landmark, the engineer tending the throttle and watching the rails saw a blue lantern, gyrating wildly beyond the curve ahead. "Damn!" he cursed, and with no other choice, applied the brakes attempting a full emergency stop. The train lurched from the rapid deceleration while brakes squealed.

Toby was thrown forward in his seat and knew instantly it meant trouble. He sprang to his feet, vaulted over a dislodged storage bin, and rushed to the passage door where his coach was coupled to the mail and baggage car, the brain center of the train. His familiarity with the occupants allowed him to quickly badge his entry into the car. Julie, also a recognized NP employee, followed close behind.

Mail clerks and baggage tenders in their working positions grabbed tumbling loose objects in complete surprise as the train ground to a halt just beyond the lantern waving man, who was within a few hundred yards of the blind curve ahead. At a complete stop, the chief mail clerk, advanced toward the head of the train to see why they had stopped. As he went forward, the baggage attendant nearest Toby muttered, "Oh no, I hope this has nothing to do with the gold."

Toby heard his utterance and inquired, "What gold?"

"We picked up a secret shipment of gold in Butte. It's labeled to go all the way to Boston, and no one is supposed to know what's in those heavy crates over there by the mail racks. We only have one Pinkerton Guard, and he's up front with the engine crew."

Toby's first instinct was to get himself and Julie out of the car and safely back into the coach. But another clerk had already locked the passage door. As he turned back to get the door released, three armed men entered the mail car from the front. They did not include the Pinkerton Guard. In loud voices they issued commands.

"Everybody stay where you are, and no one will get hurt. All of you over there with the baggage, get up against the wall. Stand together and don't move."

Toby stepped in front of Julie, hoping that she wouldn't be noticed. He might as well have been trying to hide a rose in a cactus patch. The three men, wildly pointing long-barreled revolvers moved toward the two wooden crates. The taller thin robber grabbed a baggage clerk and commanded him to assist in moving the crates over to the side door of the car. During his effort to slide the boxed cargo to the side, the bandit's scarf face mask dropped below his chin. As he grabbed it, pulling it back up, he exposed his neck, revealing a mottled messy scar. Toby immediately recognized Scar-neck, from head to heels. At the same time, the despised thief recognized Toby and knew he had been identified. The recognition of Scar-neck caused Toby to quickly assess the second man. Grey hair, stocky build, tan hat, maybe forty years old; yes boys, here is also your butchering cattle rustler.

Scar-neck forced the side door open, where a small freight wagon had been driven next to the tracks and was waiting for the cargo. The third robber appeared to be young and much frailer than the other two. Toby could not see who was driving the wagon. Toby stood silently by, watching, not wanting to attract any attention to himself or Julie. For a brief minute, the trio was vulnerable while they were struggling with the crates. Scar-neck, who was obviously in charge regained his position by ordering two of the clerks to assist in placing the crates into the wagon.

Just when Toby thought the gang would begin their escape, Scar-neck turned to Toby, pushed him aside and held his gun to Julie's head. His words were just what Toby feared, "You two are coming with us."

Toby stepped so close to Scar-neck, the bandit realized he could be in danger of losing his gun to Toby, causing him to redirect the barrel of his revolver to Toby's chin. His orders were, "Back off Junior, or you will be the first person I'll plug."

Toby said firmly, "You don't need her, I'm the one who recognizes you. Leave her here."

Scar-neck sneered, "No, Mr. Big Shot. You two may be worth more to the railroad than this here gold. Now, both of you step out of here into the wagon." Then he called out to the driver, "Tie up our friends here at the hands and feet, and then tie them into the wagon so's they don't jump out." He turned to the workers still in the mail car and shouted, "Now if any of you think you should chase us with a posse, think of what it will be like when you find these two scattered piece by piece along the trail."

The two wooden crates were loaded into the wagon before the younger robber pushed Toby and Julie out of the mail car into the hands of the driver who forced them to lie flat next to the crates. He bound their feet and hands with a thin rope and for extra security, put a rope around Toby's neck. The others retrieved their horses that had been tied to a ladder near the front of the train. All left the stalled train at a fast gallop, painfully bouncing Toby and Julie in the rear of the wagon.

As the wagon bounced over the rough ground Toby struggled to roll over so he could see Julie. He finally worked himself around to where he could see her head bouncing near one of the crates. Her hat fell onto the wagon bed, but she managed to grab it in her teeth and work it under her face to prevent the rough boards from abrading her already scratched chin. She shouted something to Toby, but the noise of the bounding wagon drowned out her voice.

Finally after a half mile of dangerous speed, the group was out of view from the railroad and heading toward the Yellowstone River, a short distance to the north. With the slower pace, Toby was able to get his bearings and assess their predicament. He and Julie were now hostage to four train robbers; not as a planned act, but as a convenient insurance for their safety. It was plainly evident that Scar-neck realized Toby had recognized him, and to prevent being identified he had to remove Toby from the scene, neutralize him as a witness, either by killing him right there or waiting until there were no other eyes to see his demise. He shuddered to think of what terrible things might lie ahead for Julie. Toby was already thinking of ways to save Julie and himself from death at the hands of these men of no conscience.

Lying in the wagon, there was no opportunity to escape. His hands and feet were bound and still had a rope around his neck snugged to a floorboard ring. He knew he must develop a dialogue to delay his demise. Emerging as most important was Scar-neck's statement that he and Julie might be worth as much as the gold. He had to make the gang believe the NP would pay a great sum for their safety; although he knew Scar-neck would never deliver him safely back to civilization to testify about his bad deeds. A quick look at Julie communicated that she too knew her future was not promising.

The wagon slowed and rolled through tall grass that appeared to be river bottom. Julie could see tall cottonwoods towering over the wagon after she managed to twist onto her back. Her chin stung from scraping on the rough boards, but it did not feel like it was openly bleeding. She understood they had been kidnapped, in what was supposed to be a robbery. The exchange between Toby and the gang leader had not gone unnoticed. There was bad blood between them that did not just sour today. She too, hoped they would both be held unharmed to enable the gang to collect a ransom, but had little faith they would be released to become witnesses.

Toby, unable to sit up because of the rope around his neck, could only rely on his senses to determine their location. He could hear the river nearby, and through the wagon side boards could see water rushing over the banks, drowning the petals of the blooming wild roses. The smells emerging from the flooding were pungent with pollen and drifting debris. He reasoned there was no way they would be crossing the river with the wagon, or even on horseback. Yet they were far too close to the scene of the robbery to be safely hidden. Fear gripped him. Would they dare throw Julie and him into the torrent to drown? He struggled to sit up, but couldn't.

Julie had not been tied by the neck. When the wagon stopped, she managed to twist herself up so that her back rested against the wagon side. What she saw and said calmed Toby only slightly. "Toby, they may have a boat."

The driver turned around to look at his cargo. To get room to maneuver, he released the rope from Toby's neck and allowed him to set up. The other three men also approached the wagon. The young one, now appearing to be no more than a teen, said, "Let's get a look at the gold!" With total gang approval, Scar-neck took an iron bar and pried the lid off the first crate. Inside, stacked in organized rows were standard sized gold bars, which Toby knew would measure seven inches long, three and five-eighths wide and one and three quarters thick, and weigh 439 ounces, or 27 pounds. The market price for gold was twenty dollars and sixty-seven cents per ounce, making each bar worth approximately nine thousand, seventy-four dollars. And there were a lot of them.

Each member of the gang whooped and hollered, while hefting at least one of the bars in their hands. The driver, in a Mexican accent said, "Let's look in the other one." With the lid pried off, the contents revealed something different. Several small canvas sacks were bound shut at the top and attached with a labeled tag. Scar-neck cut open the top of one of the bags and poured into his hand small particles of gold. Toby recognized it as placer gold, yet to be refined.

The robbery plan was no longer a mystery to Toby. Placer Gold was often transported to Butte for refining; however the Montana Copper Company was not yet fully operational. A small amount of smelting was done in Meadville, east of Butte. Gold was rarely transported east on the NP, but the buyers varied their methods for security. The real mystery was created by the behavior of the robbers. They knew exactly how the gold was being shipped, to include the date, time, and even how it was crated for delivery. They didn't even need to look into the crate until they were a safe distance from the train. Toby silently thought, "Angela, how about your friend in special shipments? Would it have been possible for her to have breached the security? Scar-neck was not capable of planning this by himself."

Scar-neck pounded the lid back onto the crates and motioned to the heavy-set older man, speaking his name, "Bolo, get these two bread crumbs out of the wagon, but keep their hands tied. Take them across the river to the camp. I'll stash the Gold with…well you know, and explain that we have a bonus package to deal with. Come back over and get me in about two hours. I'll be here, just across the river."

Bolo began leading his two captives toward the river, and fear again gripped Toby. Surely, they wouldn't attempt crossing the river on horseback. If the horses didn't drown, he and Julie surely would, having their hands tied. Toby was about to break his silence when he saw a boat, moored in the willows along the bank. Bolo gave instructions, "Step over there, and into the boat. The water is only about a foot deep up to the boat. If you need to, you can hang onto the rope."

The rope, Toby noticed, was actually a large cable, stretched from the south bank to a sturdy cottonwood on the north edge. The boat was tethered to an iron ring, rigged to slide along the cable, from one side of the river to the other. A system of ropes allowed the boat to be returned without passengers. The cable seemed to be only temporarily attached, allowing it to be removed, leaving no other access to where they were going.

Toby, emboldened by the absence of two of the gang objected. "I'm not getting in there with my hands tied. If we tip over, both of us will drown. And while you're at it you might as well cut our feet loose. We won't be going anywhere once we get into the boat."

Bolo thought about it for only a few seconds, and whistled to the young man and the Mexican wagon driver. Once again, a name was mentioned, "Sanchez, hold a gun on these two while I take off their ropes. Keep 'um covered until they are in the boat. Kid, you come with us, and Sanchez, you stay here and fix the line onto the ring so you can pull the boat back, and stay here until Frank gets back. Depending on what he learns, we can decide if we want to take down the cable."

The entire conversation was very revealing. Both Toby and Julie understood, this operation had been well planned, except they were now both a "bonus" and a problem.

Toby and Julie sat in the back of the boat, while Bolo and the Kid pulled on the transport line. Although the boat had oars, not one touched the water. On the other side, both were held at gunpoint until all were on dry land, and the boat was being pulled back to the south bank. The captives were in suspense as to their fate while they were being led into boulders beneath cliffs near the riverside. To their surprise, four horses were tethered out of sight among the rocks. Toby and Julie were both placed onto one horse, their hands tied, and a rope drawn around them so that they were roped together. The reins of their mount were taken by Bolo. They rode north, with the Kid traveling in the rear.

Less than a half hour passed before they reached a small shallow box canyon in the sandstone formations of the Bull Mountains. They dismounted and became the fearful guests of a cattle rustling, train robbing, kidnapping, gang of outlaws.

Toby knew there would soon be Marshals looking for them. But they would be of no help, even though they were just across the river.

Seventeen

Toby and Julie were placed on the ground, with a boulder as a backrest. Their hands remained tied, and their feet were again bound. The thieves seemed to have an abundance of rope left from picketing their horses and lashing branches for a lean-to shelter. A large fire pit dominated the center of the rectangular open-air hideaway. Blankets and bed rolls were stacked within the shelter, indicating they may have used the location before the June weather had become unseasonably warm. For now, they sat and waited.

Bolo separated Toby and Julie so they could not talk to each other, but they still had eye contact. It was midafternoon, and Toby was hoping they could somehow break away before the others arrived at the camp. He mouthed the words, "Try to get loose" to Julie.

She mouthed back, "Sure."

He communicated, "I have a knife."

She repeated a sentence several times before Toby understood, "Good. Wait until dark."

Obviously, she didn't know Scar-neck as well as Toby. He hoped to live until dark.

Finally they heard riders approaching. Bolo jogged to the canyon entry, gun in hand, only to greet Scar-neck and Sanchez.

None of their conversation was audible until they sat on stumps surrounding the fire pit.

Spoken in low tones he heard Bolo ask, "Well, what'd he say?"

Scar-neck answered, "He was pleased with the amount of gold, but was mad as hell about us taking the two railroad wimps. I had to explain who this Toby guy was and then when he understood he agreed we couldn't have him squealing out who we were. Then when we started talking about trading them back to the railroad for money, he got all happy about it."

"So now what we gonna do?" asked Bolo.

"We wait here for a couple of days while Bossman gets ahold of the Railroad. He's gonna ask for twenty thousand for the two of them. We'll arrange a payoff by train. We'll wait with a green lantern, trackside way out away from any town with a posse, and at night, so nobody can see us. When the engineer sees the lantern, he drops the money and keeps going.

"Man that sounds good. Bossman can really figger things out. That's a lot of dough! So, you think they'll pay it?"

Scar-neck lowered his voice until it was barely audible, "If they don't, we'll bury them out here in the sagebrush. If they do pay, we'll bury them anyway."

The breeze was just right to carry the sound in the late afternoon air. Toby heard it all. He could tell looking at Julie, leaning up against the large rock, that she too heard the ugly plans.

Hard times had made Toby patient. He chose to appear docile, not wanting to attract attention to himself. His greatest secret of the moment was that, according to his deceased father's instructions, he always carried a knife. That constant companion was in a custom sheath in his boot. They carelessly did not search him, and if he remained quiet, they probably would not bother. Julie was right. He would wait until after dark.

Julie, however was not being docile. Knowing that Toby would eventually go into action, she wanted to appear as though she was the most significant threat to be concerned about. She began to squirm, and announced that she needed to be free to relieve herself. At first the men laughed, but she very unshyly persisted until Scar-neck said to the Kid, "OK, untie her, and put a rope around her neck. Tie the rope to that iron pot by the fire pit so's she has to drag it. That'll keep her from runnin' away. Then let her go."

"Why can't I just follow her?", he said with offensive eagerness.

"Don't get no ideas." Bossman said we
got to keep her in good shape right up until the end in case someone needs to see she is safe before they pay. So that's the way it's gonna be. Understand?"

The dejected Kid untied Julie's legs so that she could stand comfortably. She stood a good three inches taller than him. He untied her hands and let her stretch her arms. While he was doing as told, he spoke kindly to her, showing sympathy and obviously trying to gain her favor. Seeing through his charade she responded in kind, thanking him for his gentleness. As he slipped the noose around her neck, he just couldn't resist grabbing her breast. With her arm fully extended, she spun on her feet and swung an open palm across his face and jaw that would have split a wooden block. The smack of the contact cracked like a rifle. If his jaw still hung straight, it was not her fault. Kid fell over into the dirt, landing on his side. Dazed and unable to get back on his feet, he heard the sound of laughter. All but Toby were gleefully huffing at the sight of Kid's putdown. With her despised victim still sitting in the dirt, she picked up the iron pot with one hand and stomped off behind the boulders. She could have easily clubbed the little fool with the swinging pot but knew the results would be calamitous. Escape, beyond the brush was also considered, but she would never leave without Toby.

When Julie was out of hearing range, Scar-neck warned the others. "She's mighty pretty, but she ain't no Cinder-sissy-rella. We got to keep her well till we get the money. But you seen it; she's a worry. That gal is meaner than a pup-nursing mamma wolf. You boys better leaver her tied up, and keep an eye on her. She's got a fire in her belly that will burn every one of us if you get careless."

The afternoon wore on until Sanchez built a fire and cooked the evening meal. Venison, beans, coffee and dandelion greens were served in tin cups. Julie thought how it was a giant step down from the meals she had been served the last ten days. But had she known what was ahead of her, she would have eaten more.

As a half-moon rose over their darkened camp, Kid checked both Julie and Toby to be sure their hands and feet were still bound. They were each given a blanket and made to stay on opposite sides of the fire pit. Bolo, Sanchez and Scar-neck bedded down under the lean-to, leaving Kid to take a position at the edge of the shelter to observe the hostages.

Toby waited two hours until he heard the heavy breathing and snoring of each gang member. In the past, he had freed himself from leg bondage by removing his boots. Tonight it was an easy task. With his boots removed, he slid the knife out of the lining, cut the ropes from his legs and lay back down, checking the sounds from the sleeping thieves. Satisfied, he cut free his hands, and crawled quietly to Julie. She was wide awake waiting his rescue. Not a word was spoken as he cut her free. He instinctively picked up the cut ropes. He kept one of the longer pieces, and hid the others in the sage brush, so not to disclose he had a knife. As an afterthought he rolled up Julie's blanket, tied it with the rope and slung it over his shoulder. Together they crept out of the confined stack of boulders.

Earlier, while Toby was sitting through the afternoon, he scanned the rocks above him for a hiding place. From his view below, he saw two possibilities, each requiring a steep climb, but safely away from the camp's view. Now in the darkness of a half moon, he followed his observed route. He carefully led Julie up over the rocks into a depression formed by surrounding boulders. There they stopped.

Julie whispered, "Why are we stopping here?"

Toby explained. "It's only about four hours until daylight. They'll soon notice we're gone and all hell will break loose. They'll come looking on horses spread out in every direction and we won't have a chance escaping in the daylight. If we stay here, right above them, they will never suspect we didn't run off. They won't look this close to their camp. We can hide here until tomorrow night when they come back, and leave as soon as it gets dark. That way we can get rested and have a full night of travel tomorrow; then hide again during the day."

"That sounds good, but scary to be so close all day."

"They won't be down in the camp, because they will be looking for us. Right here will be the safest place to spend the day."

"Toby, I love you. You are so smart. But where are we going to go?"

"We can't go toward the river. It's a complete barrier and they'll look there first thinking they can track us through the grass and willows. We have to outsmart them. The only direction we can go is north. They'll think it stupid to wander up there into the wilderness, but they don't know we both grew up in this country. We'll head up toward the Musselshell until we can find help."

"But Toby, it's so far."

"Yes I know. Believe me, I've been there. But Julie, it's our only chance. If these guys catch us, they plan to just use us to get a ransom and kill us afterwards."

She shuddered, "Yes, I heard that."

In the darkness, Toby smoothed the ground around them scattering lose dirt and sand to make a place to spread the blanket. In a tense setting, they waited for the morning's first light.

Eighteen

As dawn broke, they heard the commotion below. "Kid, wake up you idiot! Where's the rail bum and his fancy lady? You were supposed to keep an eye on them during the night."

Scar-neck was angrily yelling out orders. "Everybody, get a rope and saddle up. We got to find those babies or Bossman will kill us. They can't be far. On foot they can't be more than five or six miles. Bolo, you go upriver, and I'll go down. Sanchez, you work out from here looking for tracks. Kid, get your miserable ass out in the hills to the north. If anybody picks up a trail, fire three shots to signal where you are, and everybody come join in."

Scar-neck continued shouting orders, and intermittently cursing at Kid. Before leaving he said, "Everybody be back here at least an hour before sundown, because I have to meet Bossman here, and you're all gonna help me explain. He'll for sure lay out a new plan, and everybody better for sure pay attention."

He rode toward the river, still cursing at Kid.

Toby and July heard it all, and as they rode off, Toby watched to see that Kid did not look up in their direction. As Kid disappeared out of sight, and

Sanchez wandered to the east, Toby finally stretched out onto the blanket to rest. The sun was rising and he realized they were going to have another problem. It was going to be a very hot day, and they were secluded in a virtual sun baked oven.

As he lay there thinking, Julie began to slap her arms, scratch her legs and fuss about bugs. Suddenly, she said much too loudly, "Toby, get up. I'm covered with ants. Look, they're getting all over you too."

She stood up, and Toby had to grab her hand and caution her to stay low so she would not be seen above the boulders. She said, "Toby, they're starting to bite. I've got hundreds all over me."

He too was now feeling the hundreds of tiny legs crawling over his body, occasionally biting under his clothing.

"Julie, we've got to take our clothes off."

"What?"

"Take you clothes off! We have to shake them out. In the dark, I put this stupid blanket over an ant hill."

By now, the bites were becoming frequent, and she needed no more encouragement to remove her clothes. Upon doing so, she discovered there were no safe areas in her garments. She had to remove them all. Toby hardly noticed until they were both standing naked, shaking the ants out of every item worn. She looked at Toby and broke out in a hysterical giggle. She said, "If Kid discovers us like this, I'm just going to ask him to shoot me."

Toby too, found the spectacle humorous. He commented, "Well, I guess it's a good thing we got married."

She snickered, "Wait till I see the girls back in St. Paul, and I tell them what we did on our honeymoon; 'Just to get me undressed in the daylight, he spread our blanket in an ant pile.'"

In spite of the danger surrounding them, they laughed, brushing their clothes in the nude, until they were certain all ants were removed. The thought of being shot bare naked hastened their redressing. When reclothed, Toby again surveyed the area to be sure they were still alone. When safe, they shook the swarming ants off the blanket, and moved to another side of their rock hideaway. The new location did not afford as good a view of the bandit's camp, but they were certain they would be able to hear the approach of horses.

The day passed slowly. The sun bore down on them. They had no water, a miscalculation that plagued Toby in the past. He viewed the campsite from the edge of the rocks, and saw no vessel that could contain water. In addition, he dared not disturb the campsite or they would realize he and Julie had hidden close by. He considered sneaking into the camp site to steal any remaining food, but he had lost track of Sanchez. To venture out in the open, was too great a risk. He reasoned they could do without food for a couple of days. The immediate emergency was to stay alive and escape. They could eat later, but water remained an unsolved problem.

The sun bore down on them with no mercy. At midday the shadows cast by the boulders were almost nonexistent. The rocks around them grew hot to the touch, and the brightness penetrated even closed eye lids. Julie's light complexion was turning pink. Toby, seeing Julie beginning to suffer, suggested that to prevent the sun burn, she should remove the outer layers of her clothing and wrap it over her head and exposed hands.

As she unbuttoned her split skirt, she said, "There you go again Mister! Talking me out of my clothes."

They both laughed while she draped her face under the excess cloth of the skirt and Toby sat in the dirt, giving her his share of the blanket to fully cover her legs. He rested against a boulder while hiding under his hat. Late in the afternoon, the sun finally lowered into a position offering them relief. Scant shadows slowly slid out from under the giant rocks, forming pools of welcome shade.

Their comfort was brief, interrupted by the sound of horse hooves. Kid was returning. He tied his horse on a twig only fifteen feet below the hiding hostages. Toby, wary of the ants still feverishly repairing their home, watched through the windows between boulders. Kid appeared to have just come from the river. His hat and hair were wet, cooling his face, while his pants were wet around his boots. He rolled open a blanket, and lay in the shade of the shelter.

The lazy little villain snoozed only a few minutes until several riders appeared. They numbered four: Scar-neck, Bolo, Sanchez and the person who Toby recognized as Bossmiller. To his detriment, Kid did not wake on their arrival. Low mumbling was heard from the group until Scar-neck strode to Kid's side and kicked him in the belly. Kid rolled into a ball and screamed in pain. Bolo grabbed him by his shirt and stood him up.

With much cursing, Scar-neck said, "What are you doing here sleeping after you let two witnesses and twenty thousand dollars run into the bushes? You ain't even worth beating the crap out of."

The kid finally getting back his breath said, "OK then, I'll leave. You can just give me my share of the gold, and you all can have the rest."

Scar-neck glanced at Bossmiller who nodded negatively, side to side. Bossmiller then took control. He directed his voice toward Bolo, who was standing next to Kid, "He seems to like the river. Take him down for a swim."

Bolo, a strong man, tucked Kid's head under his arm in a hammer lock, and drug him into the trees beyond the camp. Kid's screams were audible while he was being dragged toward the river. The pleas became fainter until two shots in succession echoed through the rocks, and all was quiet. Bolo returned alone in less than an hour, and made no mention of Kid.

The four men remained in camp for the rest of the evening. They discussed their fortunes and misfortunes. Bossmiller took a bottle of whiskey from his saddle pack and they celebrated their new ill-gained riches. A discussion followed, all about making assignments and plans to locate Julie and Toby. With whiskey fueled cursing and high volume they blamed the hostages' escape and all of their misfortunes on Kid. Toby and Julie were thankful for the volume, because they heard all of the search plans, and made their own accordingly.

Bossmiller did not plan to participate in the search. He said, "They can't get anywhere on their own. They won't be able to cross the river for another month. You be sure you disable the boat crossing after I leave. The only place they can cross now is up at Huntley or at Billings. They'll probably try for that because it's too far downriver before they can get anywhere, and its rough country besides. That's why we made that our stash. If they go north, it's forty miles before they find help unless they find cowboys with a herd. But I don't think we can rule that out, because that guy is smart. You may not like him Frank, but the guy is smart. He'll make a fool out of you if you aren't really careful. He had you figured out in the card game within the first hour. His advantage in going north is there's a whole lot of country out there. You could hide a herd of buffalo out there and ride right past 'um. His disadvantage is, new fresh grass leaves a trail."

Bossmiller paused for a drink and passed around the bottle. He continued uninterrupted, "So here's what I think we should do. I'll go back across the river and deal with the railroad. Bolo, you and Sanchez go west upriver looking for a trail. Go as far as Huntley and ask around at the crossing to see if they've been there. If not, come on back and we'll decide whether to search east, or join up with Frank to the north. They won't survive long out there alone, and somewhere they're going to have to show themselves."

Bolo coughed and replied, "I don't know. The guy is smart, and that little missy is plain tough. Did you see how she knocked Kid on his ass? That was funnier than a clown rodeo."

Scar-neck, Frank, said, "Yah, maybe, but I been wanting to pay him back for a long time. I owe him one, and I intend to find him, and little missy will just be a bonus."

Toby and Julie watched as they talked until dark, finished the bottle and bedded down under the shelter. Toby noticed they had not released Kid's horse, nor gathered up any of his belongings. Unfortunately most of them, including his saddle, were lying next to the shelter, but Toby spotted his canteen hanging on a bush next to the horse.

Toby whispered, "I think it's time to make our move. But we must have water! I am going to take the chance and get that canteen. We'll go down together, but you wait near the bottom so that if they wake up and chase me, you can get back up here and hide. If that happens, I will circle around, get with you and we'll go from there. If something happens to me and you end up alone, work your way upriver to Huntley, cross the river there with the bargeman, and find safety in the NP depot."

Julie said nothing, other than to nod her head.

Toby crept toward the camp in the dim light, carefully placing each step to prevent noise. He slowly removed the canteen from the bush and was elated to find it full. He lifted it to his side and carefully walked around the rump of Kid's horse, a strong looking grey. Two steps beyond, he had an idea, that changed his plans. He looked at the intoxicated robbers, slumbering twenty paces from him. He could take this horse with him unnoticed. The reins, loosely wrapped around a sage branch were silently unraveled. He quietly patted the horse's neck and gently led the horse toward Julie's hiding place among the rocks. He did not dare to lead the horse completely up to Julie, for fear the horse would stumble on a rock or noisily kick one free to roll toward the camp. He stopped five paces from where Julie should have been hiding and waited. She did not appear. As he waited in the dark, he could hear nothing, not even the snoring of the men. He remembered a night birds whistle that he and Julie imitated, playing together as children.

Julie saw the horse approaching in the darkness. Terribly frightened, she thought it might be one of the bandits, patrolling the camp. She froze next to the boulder as the horse stopped only a few steps from her. What could the rider be looking at? Where was Toby? She waited, barely breathing. Then she heard the song of the night bird; the imperfect imitation by Toby. She rose to see the horse had no rider.

She slowly crept to the front of the horse, to find Toby holding the reins. Startled and confused, she whispered, "What are you doing with this horse?"

Just as she uttered her whispered question, they heard loud coughing from the shelter, now only thirty paces away. The coughing continued until they heard movement, and a man clearing his throat. Through the dim slivers of moonlight, Toby saw Bolo standing up, walking away from the shelter. He was walking tenderly, without his boots.

Toby put his free hand on Julie, and whispered, "Get with me in front of the horse, and don't move."

They watched as Bolo light footed his way past the fire pit, stopping very close to where the horse had been tied. There, Bolo relieved himself, and without noticing the horse was gone, turned back toward the shelter. Toby and Julie stood motionless until all of the heavy breathing resumed.

As they began to slink away from the camp, Toby whispered, "You forgot the blanket!"

Julie gasped, and Toby said, "Here, hold the horse and I'll get it." As he reached the rocks, he heard the coughing again." It was a worrisome sound but he hoped they were far enough away to continue a silent retreat. He grabbed the blanket bundle and returned to Julie,

When he returned to her touch, she was extremely upset. She could barely hush her voice as she exclaimed, "Tobias, what are you doing with this horse? They will know we took it and are still nearby!"

"I don't think so. Let me explain. The other horses are loose; out grazing. This one was poorly tied and could have easily pulled free to join them.

When they find he is gone, they may be delayed by looking for him. They will no doubt follow his tracks, and soon suspect someone has stolen him, but there are still a few bands of Sioux and Crow roaming the area and stealing horses. They won't change their plans for attempting to find us. Scar neck will follow our trail, but that's OK, because he will be coming in our direction anyway. The horse will allow us to get a good head start; far enough that the searchers won't be able to return to their camp for the night. They'll probably stay separated. We'll throw in some diversionary tricks, and abandon the horse long before daylight. That will give us time to find a hiding place for tomorrow. They won't be sure if the horse wandered away, or if we took him. Here, let me help you up, and we'll ride double, following the North Star."

"But Toby, where shall we go?"

"There's safety just across the river. But we can't get there."

"We know the country up north. I think we are about two days from the cave where I survived the winter of 1881. If we can make it to there, we can defend ourselves." He did not mention how.

Nineteen

Eddy was at the Miles City train depot to greet Toby. He rode his own horse and borrowed two from his friend Jim Little Bear. He couldn't wait to greet the two newlyweds and later introduce them to the lady who was becoming his new love.

The train was late, and Eddy impatiently paced the depot platform looking for signs of the approaching locomotive. Finally it chugged into the station. The first thing he observed was the frantic actions of people in the mail car. Three of them bolted from the train and ran into the Depot Agent's office. The conductor opened the passenger coach doors, but only three people emerged, none of them were his expected guests.

Eddy, being acquainted with most of the train personnel, approached the conductor and asked, "Hey, what's going on? Where's the rest of your passengers?"

"Oh, Mister Eddy, it's terrible. We been robbed. Four masked bandits snatched the gold shipment and took Mr. Hawthorn and Miss Julie with them."

Eddy was shocked. "Where did this happen?"

"Mister Eddy, I'm not sure. We was past the Pomp's Rock, but not quite to the Custer siding. It was somewhere around there. They had a wagon and loaded up the two crates of gold, and took Mister Hawthorn and Miss Julie with them. And I understand they had just gotten married. The leader said he would kill them both if anyone tried to follow."

Eddy needed to hear no more. He ran into the depot telegraph office and found the telegrapher already tapping the news to headquarters and all surrounding stations. When he was finished, Eddy asked if he had notified their Superintendent, Mr. Hanson. When the clerk replied yes, Eddy said, "Good, now let's send him another one. Take this down. 'TOBY AND JULIE NOW IN REMOTE TERRITORY UNFAMILIAR TO MOST. REQUEST AUTHORIZATION TO PURCHASE PACK MULE AND EQUIPMENT. WILL FOLLOW TRAIL WITH PROFESSIONAL TRACKER. SUSPECT ROBBRY BY PERSONS MENTIONED IN TOBY'S LAST REPORT. DO NOT PAY RANSOM. ROBBERS WILL KILL ALL WITNESSES AFTER PAYOFF. WILL FOLLOW UNTIL FOUND. AND REPORT WHEN POSSIBLE. EDDY KINGSTON.'"

The telegram went immediately, but Eddy waited for forty-five minutes for an answer. He expected an argument and got it. But Eddy, not to be discouraged, sent two additional messages convincing headquarters that his response would be the quickest and most flexible. They knew Eddy was a tough and reliable man, very close to both victims.

They agreed to allow his co-workers to run operations in Miles City until he returned. After several admonitions to proceed with caution, Eddy received the allowance he needed to outfit himself and Jim Little Bear for the expedition.

He took possession of Julie's and Toby's clothing and personal items that had been left on the train. He glanced through Eddy's papers, but found nothing new that could possibly be related to the recent robbery. He looked at the setting sun and knew he would have to wait until tomorrow to assemble the food, first aid and survival items needed for possibly four people. He still had time tonight to find Jim, and explain a few things to his friend Alice.

There was not time for a full history and background presentation providing a reason for Eddy's quick and passionate response to the kidnapping of his friends. He stopped by Alice's house to report he would be gone for a few days, and told her briefly why. Alice understood Eddy, and knew he would stop at nothing to help his long-time friends. He received only a few loving words of advice.

"Eddy, be careful. Do not add yourself to the fatality list that is bound to grow from this. Timmy and I have grown very fond of you, and Timmy is not ready to endure the loss of another person who he looks upon as his father."

The statement caused Eddy to pause, and ask a personal question he never felt familiar enough in their relationship to ask. "You and Timmy say that his father was killed in the Army, but you have never told him where, or how. Why not?"

"Timmy's mother died of smallpox when he was very young. His father did his best to care for him in her absence. Two years after she died the tragedy of his father's death followed. How do you tell a nine-year-old boy that his father was shot while in bed with his superior officer's wife?"

Eddy said, "Ok, enough said. I understand."

Alice finished with, "I took responsibility for him, and my father left us this little house. Timmy can call me 'Mom' as long as he wants...because he needs to. Eddy, as you know, he longs for more than that. He has endured many losses in his young life. Neither he, nor I could suffer another."

Eddy nodded, and kissed her goodbye.

* * * * *

Eddy found Jim at his secluded old log cabin, situated near the railroad bridge. Jim too was fond of Toby, and as the problem was being explained, Jim already began gathering the items he would need for this journey. They agreed to meet the next morning at the livery stable, where Eddy would be loaned, or if necessary, purchase a mule to pack their supplies.

Eddy reasoned they would need food and survival equipment for himself, Jim, and hopefully Toby and Julie. He expected to find them captive somewhere near where they were taken; perhaps just across the river, on the north side of the Yellowstone. He had no idea who robbed the train, but was even more puzzled why someone would take Toby and Julie with them. He kept asking himself, "How did Toby get put in that position?" His only answer was that Toby knew them, and had to be silenced. "And Julie, why was she taken?" She must have been nearby and an attractive convenience. Both he and Toby knew, the worst villains plaguing the railroad were Scar-neck and Bossmiller.

By morning Eddy had arranged for the early freight train to stop in Miles City. But much to his dismay it was not trailing an empty cattle car as he had requested. He was told he had to wait until tomorrow before the next train would arrive with one from Bismarck.

One more day passed with Eddy completing arrangements and working with the NP to learn anything new. Jim complained loudly that they were now a day behind, but there was nothing more Eddy could do. The entire NP organization was expecting a message from the kidnappers, but none had arrived.

By the morning of the second day after the robbery, an empty cattle car was on the sidetrack, loaded with two horses and a pack mule, along with food, water, bed rolls, rifles and first-aid supplies. A ramp was included to allow unloading the animals at any place along the track.

As the train was coupled to the car, Eddy and Jim climbed in with the animals and prepared for their short ride. The engineer of the train had been educated as to where the robbery had occurred. As they rattled out of Miles City, Eddy conferred with Jim about his plan.

It had only been two days since the robbery, so the trail should be still visible. Jim would track the wagon, and Eddy would explore anything breaking away from the trail. Together they would observe the scene and develop a plan. They both believed the rescue would have to employ stealth. An open confrontation with four armed kidnappers, would surely be detrimental to the hostages.

* * * * * * * *

One Hundred-twenty miles to the west, at a small freight stop called Clermont, midway between the Huntley and the Pompey's river crossing, a man stood across the tracks from the train depot. He studied the quiet little building at the edge of the steel rails. It was a lonesome looking little place, out in the middle of the unsettled valley. Only a few small structures dotted the dry earth, and nothing waited on the depot platform for the local homesteaders. An occasional dust devil spun circles across the flat landscape, pushing tumbleweeds into pockets of sagebrush. A row of planks positioned between the rails allowed wagon traffic to rattle across the tracks near the depot.

The man would not be known by any who might have passed. His appearance did not fit the landscape. He was tall and heavy. The wide brim of his hat, barely shaded his pox marked face and big nose. His puffy looking stomach, soft hands, as well as his woolen pants and vest, exposed him as a non-laboring man. His "City slicker appearance" set him apart, an outsider, waiting and watching next to his horse for no visible reason.

A young boy played near a trash pile, on the left side of the man's big chestnut gelding. The little lad had fashioned a stick horse from the trash, and was dodging among the tumble weeds as if he were on a cutting horse, moving cattle. As he dared to venture near the man, the big guy called out, "Hey kid, that horse got a name?"

The boy anxious to talk with someone said, "Not yet, he was just borned this morning."

The stranger advanced the conversation, "Well then, what's your name?"

"Alfred, but they just call me Little Al. They call me Little Al because my dad's Big Al, and my grandpa's Old Al."

"H-m-m, Little Al, how would you like to earn fifty cents?"

"Sure, but doin' what? My dad says I can't ride horses alone yet."

"No little man, all I want you to do is take this message over and give it to the Station Master at the Depot."

"Gee, sure I can do that."

The man took a coin from his pocket and placed in the boy's hand saying, "OK then, now listen to me. I want you to give this paper to the man, I mean the boss who runs the depot. I want to see how fast you can give it to him and leave. I don't want you to talk to him, just give him the note and run. OK? Now if you do that, and run fast, I'll give you another fifty cents when you get back."

"OK Mister. I'll leave my horse here. I can run faster without him."

The little fella ran across the tracks and disappeared into the depot. He ran up to the station master, and gave him the folded paper and started to leave. But Old Al, the man in charge said, "Just a minute Little Al, let's see what this says."

"But grandpa, the man said I had to hurry."

"And I said wait just a second."

Old Al opened the paper and read:

"To NP. We got both of them. If you want them to live, put twenty thousand in a mail bag, and onto a train. Watch at night for a green lantern between Clermont and Custer. Toss the money at the lantern and keep going. When we get the money, you get them back. You got two days. Don't wait to long. No funny stuff."

Old Al couldn't see across the tracks from his office. He told Little Al, "OK, run back over there and get a good look at the guy, but don't get close to him. I want you to come back and tell me everything you know and can see about him. OK, now git."

As Little Al trotted across the tracks, anxious to get another coin, he saw the man already mounted, turn his horse and gallop away toward the east. The youngster stopped and kicked at the trash pile, saying aloud, "It's just like grandpa says, 'Don't trust strangers for nothing, never.'"

Old Al immediately sent the message to NP Headquarters by telegram. He noticed that the wrong spelling of the word too was used. He corrected it in the telegram message.

* * * * * * * * *

It was not long before Eddy and Jim were cinching up the pack mule, the last to be unloaded. The train pulled away and they began their search on the north side of the tracks, toward the west because that was the reported direction of the wagon. Within a hundred paces, they found the trackside trampled and wagon tracks in plain view. Jim fluidly followed the tracks to the flooding river where they stopped to observe many footprints. Jim said, "They unloaded here. There are five different men's prints, and one very different one which must be Julie's."

Her prints were the easiest to follow. They led into water at the edge of the river. For a moment Eddy was taken over by fear. "My God, did they drown them?"

Jim was silent. He examined the grass and saw the trampled effect near the trees that bore the cable. On the tree bark he noticed scrape marks. With his feet in the water he could see the depression made by the bow of the boat. He said, "No, they pulled a boat across the river. They are now on the other side. But first we must find the wagon."

They rode only a quarter of a mile downstream where the wagon tracks ended. The wagon was abandoned near the riverbank. Tracks indicated one animal, probably a mule was waiting at the wagon stop. Jim speculated it was a pack mule because its smaller tracks were deeper from additional weight on departure. The two horses drawing the wagon, left with the mule, and all continued downstream to the east. Eddy said, "OK, that's where the gold went. Let's go find our friends."

Jim spoke quietly, "If they crossed the river, we can do nothing quickly. Perhaps we should follow the mule to whoever remains on this side. If we find a man at the end of the trail, we can persuade him to share his knowledge. It may be a faster way."

Eddy agreed, knowing that his anxiety was setting aside good reasoning and planning. They followed the mule trail for almost five miles until it disappeared into a flooded slough. During the night, the rising and falling water erased all traces of the tracks. On the other side of the backwater, they could see a steep grade of rocky trail. Apparently, the mule leader intended to eliminate his tracks. The time spent had not been wasted. They would remember the location for later.

The partners returned to the boat site and studied both sides of the river. Even with the high water, the landing to the north side could easily be determined, again from the crushed weeds and grass. But there was no boat in sight. Eddy made a quick decision, "We can't do anything 'till we get to the other side. I know the area. The closest crossing is at Huntley, at least twelve miles upriver."

Jim said, "Yes, I know it too. This is the land of the Crow people. The river is very strong. Not even a buffalo would swim it now."

Without further discussion, they rode toward Huntley.

The pack mule was necessarily slow, and darkness came before reaching Huntley. They spent the night near the mosquito infested river and began again at daylight.

In Huntley, the Yellowstone crossed the valley, by flowing south to north. At the edge of town, a barge attached to a cable was the only crossing for miles. The person owning and operating the ferry told them he would not load the barge with three horses during flood stage. He announced that in fact he didn't want to cross at all until the water level dropped. He said it was too dangerous and the fast current was likely to pull the already submerged cable pilings from their moorings. After much pleading from Eddy, the old man agreed to attempt the crossing in the early morning hours the next day after the temperature during the night reduced the flow. Eddy and Jim could do nothing but discuss their plans and wait until morning.

At midafternoon, Eddy examined the river flow, and noticed it was slowing slightly and the flood line along the bank had receded. He found the old man, and checked his attitude. He grumbled, "You fellers are all in a hurry. Yesterday two fellers came to the other side and kept waving at me until I crossed empty, expecting to bring them back. All they wanted to know is if another feller and his wife had crossed in the last day or so. When I told him no, they both got on their horses and left; didn't give me a dime for my trouble."

Eddy, excited by the statement, asked, "Did they describe the two they were looking for?"

The barge owner said, "He just said they were young, the man tall, and the girl was good lookin' with blond hair. Said they were friends and suppose to meet up. So now you just settle in. I can't ever remember the river being this high late in June. It's just been too dad-blamed hot. I'll take you and your friend across in the morning. Maybe if the river lowers a little, we can make it in one trip."

Eddy returned to Jim to tell him the news. "It sounds like Toby and Julie escaped. There were two men on the west side of the river asking about a couple fitting their description. It has to be our bandits, guessing Toby would try to get back to a town. Both he and Julie are smarter than that. I'm sure they are out there north of the river."

Eddy said to Jim, "Let's go over to the Huntley Depot and see if they have information about the robbery, or anything else important. They were supposed to keep all stations along the rail line on alert."

The Huntley Depot agent was wary of Eddy and Jim. He asked several questions to be sure they represented the NP. When satisfied, he produced two telegrams, one containing the ransom note. Eddy looked grim as he read it and asked, "When did you get this message?"

The telegrapher answered, "The demand was dropped off at the Clermont Station yesterday, and I got it later in the day."

Eddy's comment was short. "Send a message back to the origin of this one. DO NOT PAY. IN PURSUIT. EDDY

Twenty

Toby and Julie rode silently into the night. But he did not guide the horse in a straight line. He wobbled aimlessly at times, making the trail appear as if the horse was riderless and free to graze. Julie complained that they could make faster time walking, but Eddy reminded her that they would need to save their energy for the next couple of days when they had no choice but to walk.

Within two hours of diversionary tactics, the horse disclosed a devastating detail they had missed. The animal began limping, and soon was struggling to put full weight on his foreleg. Toby dismounted and inspected the hoof. There was nothing there to cause the lameness, but further up, the canon and knee were swollen. The animal was irredeemably lame.

Now he realized why Kid came back to camp early, and why he took a nap while the others were out searching. His horse went lame, and he could ride no further.

Both dismounted. It was several hours until daylight and they had to keep moving. Fortunately a large outcropping of rock appeared on their right. Once there, they could walk on stone to prevent leaving a shoe print trail. They both climbed back onto the horse, and forced him to walk another hundred paces to large boulders at the base of the sandstone bluffs. They stepped off onto a flat boulder. Toby swatted the horse who was eager to separate himself from his burden. As the horse limped into the night, Toby muttered, "He was partially responsible for Kid's death, but he isn't going to cause ours."

In the dim light, they made their way on the rocks above the grass for several hundred yards, until it was impossible to advance without walking on earth. Back on the ground, Toby led the way, zigzagging through the greasewood and sagebrush. They continued until fingerlings of dawn light began gripping the hills, warning them that they must secrete themselves in shelter for the day.

Again, Toby chose the high ground. They had been following a sandstone ridge that produced a castle like top from which they could see a great distance. Toby climbed the ridge first to determine if they would have shade from the hot summer sun. Several shallow wind scarps provided shade and seclusion. The pair worked their way into the rocks where they found relief. They were several miles from the abandoned horse, and had left very little shoe prints for even the best of trackers to follow.

They barely settled onto their spread blanket when Julie said, "Do you realize that we haven't eaten in two days? My stomach sounds like an old bugle."

Toby sighed, "I was thinking the same thing."

"We can't go on without eating something."

"I have been looking, and thinking as we walked. There are plenty of rabbit trails in the brush. Maybe I could make a snare."

"Out of what?"

"We have that piece of rope tied around the blanket. I could unravel the strands to make a snare loop, and rig it up with sage brush. Then there's always snakes to be found around these rocks. They'll come out in the daytime."

Julie groaned, "Ugh, I hate snakes! But I am so hungry! Remember that little store next to Aunt Rosie's house? I could eat aisles two and three."

Toby lamented, "To make matters worse, we are out of water. There're only a few drops left. I studied a map of this area with Eddy, when I was showing him how I got to the Yellowstone from Musselshell. I know there are several creeks which we should be crossing. Most of them run toward the Yellowstone, from northwest to southeast. Tomorrow we can head straight north and should be crossing some of them. I hope they haven't all dried up for the summer. You just have to think about other things and the hunger isn't so bad."

"I suppose. At first, I was too scared to be hungry. When they killed Kid, the sound of it almost made me throw up. I didn't like him, and he was stupid. The poor kid didn't know if he lost his horse or found a rope. But to hear him being killed has shaken my soul. I keep hearing him pleading, even when I try to sleep. Toby I am still so very scared. This is supposed to be our honeymoon. At least three men out there are looking to kill us. If they find us, we're as good as dead. I know Toby, if they find me, I will be wishing I was dead before it's over."

Toby knew she was telling the truth. He wondered if he would be the first to die, or would he be forced to see her tortured to death. He tried to divert her attention. "As soon as I can see, I will braid this rope into a snare loop. I'll go down to the rabbit trails and set the trap. There may be enough rope for two snares. You keep watch from up here, and give me the bird whistle if you see anything that even looks like a human coming our way."

The journey to the level of the sagebrush was much quicker than the previous trip to the top. Toby set the snare, skeptical that it would catch anything during the light of day. As he was climbing back up the rocky path the sun was already warming the rocks. He was thinking of ways to shelter from the heat, when he halted stone still. The head of a rattlesnake glanced by the outside of his right boot. The striking viper either missed, or glanced off the boot. Toby jumped to the side, avoiding a second strike, but could find no other defense. He retreated to a level of rocks slightly higher than the snake, grabbed a piece of dead pine branch and called for Julie.

Weary from the night's travel, she did not respond quicky until Toby cautioned, "Don't come any closer! There's a big rattler just below me."

"What do you want me to do?" she shrieked.

"I'll pin him with this stick. You then hold him down with the stick while I get a rock big enough to kill him."

"No, you hold him while I get the rock."

As she spoke, Toby had the stick in place wedging the coiling, writhing snake into a rock crevasse. The viper wiggled and twisted too much for her to aim her fist sized rocks effectively. The diamond shaped patterns on his wrist-sized torso rose and fell like a bull whip, while the tail buzzed a warning. She frantically said, "Get him out here where I can hit his head."

Toby loosened the pressure on the stick, and the snake struck at the boot again, still falling short. He recoiled to strike a third time when Julie flattened his head with the first rock. The second rock landed further down the snake's neck and finally slowed his resistance. Toby drew his knife and severed the snake's head, being careful not to get bitten by the still active jaws.

Julie sat back as if she had just fought a war. "I told you. I hate snakes!"

"Yup, that's why I killed it." He looked at her and grinned. "You did a great job. Now we can eat it."

"You've got to be kidding. How do you cook a snake? Maybe if I close my eyes; I'm so hungry I can almost eat anything."

"Unfortunately, I don't think we can risk a fire up here to cook anything. Just a little smoke will give away our position."

"Eat it raw? Awk, I'll gag!"

Toby cooled the conversation with his slow low tone. "I'll skin it, cut it up, and set the pieces out on a rock to slow cook and dry. When the sun's straight up, you can fry an egg on these rocks. By afternoon it may be delicious. Now before it gets too hot, I'm going back down the other side because I saw a damp spot that may contain water under the surface."

In a short while, Toby returned with the canteen half full of water. He dug a hole in the gravel and slowly strained a few handfuls through his shirt. He said, "You may get a little sand in your teeth, but it's wet." Julie was still disturbed over the snake, but they both drank and settled in the shade to rest.

By four in the afternoon now Sunday, June twenty-seventh, they had been captive or fleeing, since the robbery on the Friday afternoon of June twenty-fifth. It was over a hundred degrees and the rock hideout was radiating stifling heat. Their last real meal had been breakfast on the Friday train ride. Toby gathered up the snake "steaks" that had been baking in the sun, and said, "I think we better eat these. They actually appear to be baked." It was a big snake and there was plenty for each. Julie looked at it for a minute and watched Toby eat his first piece. He pretended that it was good. She knew better, but said, "Well, I am really hungry."

Toby gave her the best cooked and most tender piece he thought was available. She closed her eyes, put it in her mouth, chewed twice and swallowed. She started to gag, but opened her eyes and took a deep breath. "I guess I am really hungry", she said, and ate another five pieces.

They rested until an hour after sundown.

Twenty-one

The old raft operator had Jim and Eddy across the Yellowstone by mid-morning. Three days had passed since the robbery. This was beginning the fourth. Both were anxious to gallop back to the Pompey's river crossing, but they proceeded cautiously, not knowing where their adversaries might be secluded. Eddy knew if he ran into Scar-neck, he and Jim would be recognized immediately. The first to shoot would be the only survivors. They set their pace, keeping the mule pack animal at a brisk walk. They approached each outcropping of rock carefully, separating themselves, trying not to be an easy target. The sun was on its downward arc when they arrived at the banks of the Pompey's Pillar crossing.

Jim could still easily interpret the tracks. They showed multiple people traversed in all directions, and several riders had gone north, away from the river. Whatever was used to cross the river was now gone. Obviously, a boat was used to cross from the south side, to waiting horses on the north bank. Both decided that a camp lay ahead and waited until dusk to follow the trail.

They crept into the camp, only to find it empty. Eddy made an encouraging discovery. A short piece of rope sharply cut on both ends, fortified his belief his friends had escaped.

Once again, they had to prudently wait. The horses needed rest, tracking would be difficult at night, and their lack of visibility would make them vulnerable to those who must still be searching or perhaps hiding in the area.

By sunrise, five days after the robbery, Jim began tracking. It took an hour to determine two riders had gone to Huntley and returned. It confirmed their belief that their friends had escaped. One of the two who traveled to Huntley, departed toward the east, probably because they had now eliminated the western route to Huntley. The second followed a trail toward the north, away from the river. Jim felt there were three horses traveling north. They held hope the riders were Scar-neck, plus one of the riders returning from Huntley, and hopefully Toby and Julie on the third.

Again they proceeded cautiously, avoiding open spaces and blind rock outcroppings.

Twenty-Two

Toby was now navigating by the stars, and dead reckoning. On this second night of travel, he planned to cross the grassy flat to his left which would take them west into the next range of cliffs and pines. According to his memory of the maps, they should come across at least one creek during the night.

Moonlight was getting dimmer with the waning stages of the lunar cycle. Although the moonlight was fading, the stars snuck into the blackness and flickered brighter. The night air was cooler, with puffy breezes tipping sagebrush tops in the starlight. Walking through the sage and cactus was becoming more difficult. Sage crowns softly reflected the dim light, but stretches of dark green grass suspended their feet in blackness. Toby led the way in his thicker boots, knowing snakes still lurked in the dry brush; but they were heartened to know they were less vulnerable with each night of lunar progression. Toby hoped to reach their intended destination in the next two days. Just before climbing the cliffs, housing his favorite cave, they would have to cross an open grassy valley. Darkness would protect them, but in the dark, ground hazards were well hidden, plus, it was much harder to walk without leaving tracks. They had to step wherever there appeared to be solid footing. This night, with their eyes adjusted, they made good progress.

When they had crossed the little valley between the ridges, they heard the sound of running water. A rivulet of fresh water was flowing from the very last of the winter store. At the edge of the shrunken little creek, they drank, filled the canteen, and rested.

Julie sighed, "Toby, even though I am scared, I love this. The sky is beautiful holding up that ragged little piece of moon. The air is clean. I can smell the grass, and we don't have to look up to see the clouds, even at night. I miss this. Last night was the first time I saw a falling star in years. I am so glad we are sharing this now. If I have to die, I hope it's out here in the heart of nature."

Toby put his arm around her and softly said, "Julie, we are not going to die out here. I sense that we may live out here again, hopefully seeing many falling stars and changing moons. I've told you very little about the cave we are headed for, but there will be security there until we can be found."

"But who will find us?"

"Eddy knows. I can feel his presence coming. I can't explain it Julie. It's not just hope. I believe it. I can feel him coming."

"I have great faith in you both, and my parents taught me to survive out here too. I feel better now that I have water and have eaten that wonderful snake. Ugh! You're right, I shall be stronger. OK, get up, let's get going."

Toby never, ever felt Julie was a burden. Instead, she was an equal, courageous, brave, and strong.

They walked through the night. Late, with the fading moon still visible, Toby quickly turned to take Julie's hand and said, "Get down, sit next to me in this bush."

"What's happening?" she asked.

"I thought I saw the moonlight flash on something bright. It came from over there, back where we were about a half hour ago. Let's sit here for a few minutes; listen and watch."

A heard of eleven deer slowly munched their way around them while the concerned humans determined there were no horses in the group.

Toby could feel Julie's heart beating through her hand. He squeezed it tight while they waited. The light breeze brushed the grass and whispered across the flat little plain. They heard only nature and their own breathing. After a few minutes of seeing nothing more, they resumed their trek, with Toby cautiously watching and stopping occasionally to listen.

At last, a glow in the east caused them to search for another place to spend the day. Another ridge, and another rock shelter; this time a place not as elevated as before, but lower in the boulders with more shade and potentially less heat, became their primitive lodging.

Julie sat on the blanket, and took off her riding boots. She said, "These boots are killing me."

"Really? Why didn't you say something before?"

"Because I thought I would die of something else before these boots caused me blisters."

"Do you have blisters now?"

"Well, a couple of little ones."

"OK, when I get back, I'll tear off a piece of my shirt and we'll wrap it around that blister. You don't want it to get any worse. We've still got a lot of walking to do."

"What do you mean? Where are you going?"

"I'm going out and set that snare again. We are going to dine well tonight. If this southeast wind continues, we can have a small fire."

Toby returned, the blanket was spread and they reclined to watch the sunrise. Julie, lying close to Toby exclaimed, "What's that crawling on your neck?"

Toby plucked the bug off and examined it. He sputtered, "It's a tick!"

Julie, expanding her view said, "Oh my gosh, there are two more on your shoulder."

Toby brushed them off, glanced at Julie and said, "And you my dear have one crawling into your hairline."

"Yaagh!, I can feel it. We are both crawling with ticks."

Toby said, "They came from the sagebrush, and we were literally sitting in it. We have to get these things off us, before they burrow into our skin. They get in and suck out blood and can really make you sick."

This time he didn't have to tell Julie she needed to disrobe. It became a race to see who could be the first to emerge nude. Julie quipped, "Do you suppose this is what Adam and Eve did on their honeymoon?"

After each item of clothing was removed, it was inspected and shaken to remove any invaders.

Toby said, "Now we have to inspect each other."

"Really?" came an indignant reply from Julie.

"Yes, these little buggers get in the warm places around your body, and burrow in. You don't even feel them digging in. Hold still, and I'll check your back and hair line. Your long hair is a place they would love."

Toby examined Julies bare back and rump. He said, "Looks OK there, now turn around."

"Toby, I am perfectly able to inspect my front side myself", but she couldn't say it without giggling.

He said, "OK, but look everywhere, like, well you know, and under your boobs."

Her response was, "OK buster, but you're next."

Satisfied that she was tick free, she turned to Toby and checked his back side. She found one working its way into his hair. Toby was in the meantime, inspecting his font. He saw a tick working its way into his navel and without realizing how it sounded he said, "Wow, come around and look at this."

Laughing out loud, Julie responded, "Oh goodie, your turn at show and tell, woo-hoo, and it's sunny side up."

They carefully worked the tick out of Toby's navel, and Julie said, "This is another great thing I must enter into my someday diary and, of course, tell the girls back in St. Paul. On our honeymoon, at four-thirty in the morning we stripped buck naked, and did a hands-on inspection for ticks."

They rested through the morning, happy in their misery.

By afternoon, the sun was scorching the landscape again. The temperature rose to over one hundred degrees and the humidity began to increase. Toby looked to the west where cumulus clouds were building.

"Julie, those clouds are building fast. I think we're going to have a thunder shower in the next couple hours. I'm going out and check those snares, and if we caught anything edible, I'll gather up some firewood. I think I can stay in among the rocks and not be seen."

He returned with a small rabbit in his hand and dry pine sticks under his arm.

"We'll have to get further back under these overhanging rocks, or get really wet. I saw a place we can keep dry, but we may not be able to build a fire there."

They carefully moved to another location with more protection from the weather, but with less visibility.

Julie said, "Don't you think that if there's a hard thunder shower, anyone looking for us, will quit their search for us and find shelter too?"

Toby agreed, but was concerned about building a fire to cook the rabbit. He skinned it, and prepared it for cooking, but placed it in a rock crevasse. Both were ravenously hungry, but not looking forward to eating the rabbit raw. Julie wisely thought it may not even be healthy. They were willing to take a major risk to have their first cooked morsels of food in four days.

Lightning split the skies while tall dark clouds dumped rain mixed with hail. The cooler air was refreshing, but it was difficult to stay dry while the wind whipped the rain in all directions. Toby filled the canteen with runoff from the rocks. He had to remove his shirt to strain the water into the canteen. The cold downpour on his bare skin was shocking and they huddled together, chilled from the rapid drop in temperature. It rained hard for a half an hour. Shortly before sunset, the clouds parted creating the largest rainbow either had ever seen. The sun was low, making the multicolored bands arch high above the little valley and anchor in the massive boulders at each end. While they marveled at the beauty, and breathed in the fresh smell of wet sage, Julie said, "I think this is a good sign. There will be happiness beyond this rainbow."

Just before sunset, Toby started a fire. The wood he sheltered from the rain was extremely dry. It burned fast and hot. He roasted parts of the rabbit on green sticks of sage, and they devoured the entire animal. He kept the fire small so that it burned with little smoke. They hoped the pungent smell of the wet sage would hide the smell of burning wood as it drifted off into the vast wilderness. Toby carefully scattered the fire ashes and removed all signs of their presence.

With their stomachs partly full of the one course meal, they readied themselves for the night's journey.

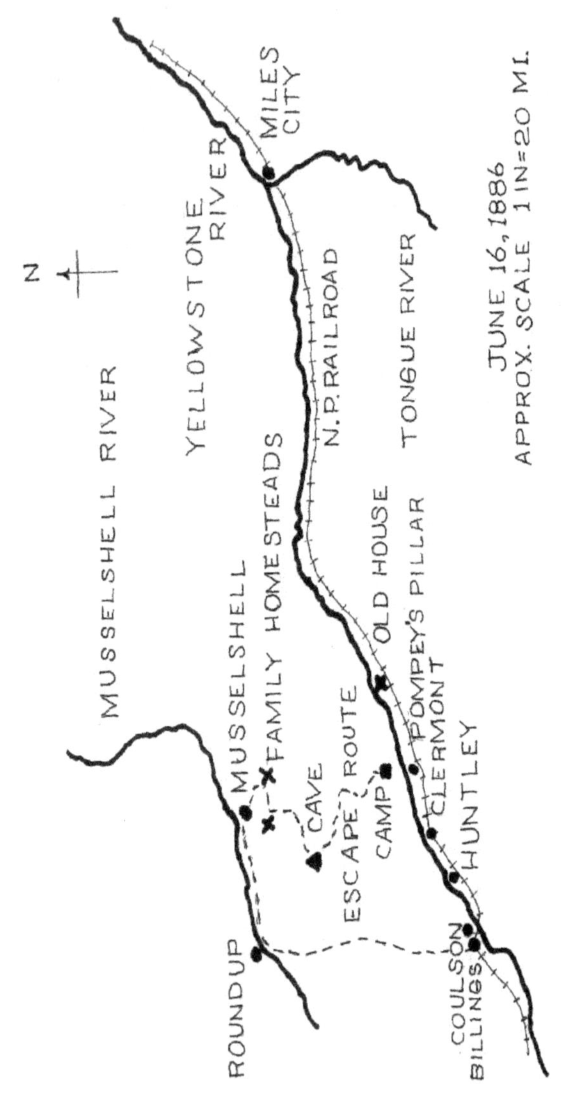
N
MUSSELSHELL RIVER
YELLOWSTONE RIVER
MILES CITY
N.P. RAILROAD
TONGUE RIVER
JUNE 16, 1886
APPROX. SCALE 1 IN=20 MI.
MUSSELSHELL
FAMILY HOMESTEADS
OLD HOUSE
POMPEY'S PILLAR
CLERMONT
HUNTLEY
CAVE
ESCAPE ROUTE
CAMP
ROUNDUP
COULSON
BILLINGS

Twenty-Three

As Toby and Julie trudged into the darkness, it was their fourth night as escapees and their third night of travel. It was obvious the journey was slowly wearing them down. Both had lost weight. Julie walked with a slight limp due to blisters from her boots. She didn't complain saying that the boots were finally getting broke-in, but Toby's own feet hurt. He realized she was suffering silently, and needed rest; time to heal. He hoped the territory he was most familiar with would soon appear out of the thickening darkness. The moon appeared only as a sliver of light, bent in a timid crescent. Luckily, the sky cleared, allowing starlight to become their only illumination. Toby wanted to cross another small valley that should bring them to the final ridge he intended to follow to his destination. At times he was able to follow game trails, hoping the heavy traffic from deer and other animals would erase their human tracks. But animals rarely chose to directly cross the little flat valleys, causing Toby and Julie to smash down the grass in their path. The signs they were leaving were definitely human.

The closer they got to their goal, the more they tried to deceive their followers. Three times during the night, Toby led Julie out into the grassy valley with both of them dragging their feet to flatten the grass in one direction. When they reached a rocky area, where normal foot traffic could be lost, they would retrace their path, but lifted their feet, carefully stepping so that they would not tip any of the grass in the direction of their retreat. When they got back to the place the deception was started, they walked over stones as far as they could, continuing north. All of the extra activity was exhausting and time consuming.

The sliver of moon had crossed the sky, and a faint hint of sunrise was showing in the east. The couple were scanning the horizon for any sign of a place to seclude themselves for the day. Hungry, and fatigued, Toby peered into the darkness ahead. There was something in the foreground, some type of small structure. They cautiously approached the low vertical image, undefined by the darkness. Toby almost shouted with surprise, "That's it! That's our wagon. Julie this is where I left our wrecked wagon, five years ago."

Toby had to make a decision. Should they travel the final two miles to the cave he knew so well? In their current condition, it would take them at least an hour to travel the distance, climb the bluffs and access the cave. Julie's only upper garment was her white blouse. It could be seen in the daylight like a lantern in the midnight green sea of grass. Yet staying near the wagon or the rocks nearby would offer little seclusion, and even greater exposure.

"Julie, it will take us an hour of hard walking to get to the cave. It will be nearly daylight before we get there. I am taking off my shirt, and you need to put it on over your blouse. My white man's skin isn't much better, but it won't stand out like that radiant white blouse. We can get there before my hide is sun blistered."

Accepting Toby's shirt she said, "The blouse is so soiled it will soon be camouflage." Then she said in jest, "Maybe I should just tramp on it a few more times."

Toby countered, "No then, Scar-neck would be able to follow us right up onto your back."

Julie shuddered, "That must not happen. Come on, let's find that cave I have heard so much about."

Toby yearned to walk the few paces to where several large stones marked his father's grave. But he did not dare to waste precious time before sunrise.

Two miles later, as he scaled the side of the bluff, Toby searched for the disheveled tree that grew in front of the cave opening. Unfortunately, many of the trees looked the same, and five years had changed the landscape. He slipped, dislodging a stone that barely glanced off Julie's shin. As he looked back, she said, "I know what you are about to say. Don't do what you've done, and leave a lot of visible marks climbing up this hill."

"Exactly," he said, and kept climbing. After ten minutes of searching, he sat on his haunches and looked out over the brightening landscape below. He remembered vividly what the scene looked like in the winter, but so much had changed. As he took in the view around him, he saw a ridge above. It was the route he used five years ago to drag his food and supplies into the cave. A little more to the west, and up another twenty feet, and he should find it. He kept scrambling.

He waited until Julie could climb to his side. Huffing from the rocky scramble, she leaned against his bare shoulder and peered into the opening. "We're going in there?" she asked hesitantly.

"Better let me look in first", he offered. "There could be all sorts of things living in there now." He added with a grin, "I haven't cleaned the place up in five years. It could have a few cobwebs."

Without taking his eyes off the opening, he said, "OK, now I am going to need my shirt."

Keeping low on his stomach, Toby crawled into the cave. As usual, it was dark inside, causing him to pause halfway through the opening. The slow entry was the most vulnerable time. Anything could attack an intruder in the face before it would be seen. When his eyes adjusted, he could see the interior, much as he remembered. It did not look as though it had been entered by humans since he left it five years prior. To his relief, he saw no sign of other animals. Wolf and his clan were gone.

Once inside, Julie was happily surprised. "Toby, this is pretty neat." "Now where's the pantry, I'm starving."

"The pantry is bare, but let me show you one of the best secrets I have been keeping."

Toby crawled on his knees to the rear of the cave where his sand bed still lay undisturbed. He dug to the side of it, and uncovered a long object wrapped in canvass. He tossed the canvas to the side, exposing a rifle, tarnished only by a few small spots of rust. The dry sand had preserved it well. Julie did not yet know that five years ago, he and the wild wolf sharing the cave, had killed the man possessing the rifle. It was a secret he vowed to keep to himself forever. But now he felt as though he and Julie were one.

He was about to tell her the story revealing how he took the rifle from "Mean Morgan", when she exclaimed, "A rifle! Fantastic! You never told me that you had two rifles and that you left one here. I guess that makes sense though, you only needed to carry your Pa's all the way to Billings. I understand now why you were so confident we could defend ourselves here. Scar-neck and his friends won't know we have a gun. That gives us the upper hand."

Julie jumped to the conclusion that he and his Pa had two guns when they crossed the wilderness. She was so filled with jubilation and excitement that Toby cowardly again chose not to tell her about the gun and Mean Morgan. He knew that if they were to live, she would soon witness death close up. Hopefully, if it happened as he planned, he could better explain then.

Toby mildly responded saying, "Yes it does, and it also will provide us something to eat. Now you put the blanket down in this little depression that I used to call my bed, and get some rest." As he reached for the box of rifle cartridges that had been wrapped with the gun, he said, "I am going out onto the far side of this rock formation and get us breakfast, dinner and supper."

She reclined and cautioned, "Won't they hear your shots and come after us?"

"They will be coming from the east, and I will be shooting on the west side. I doubt it will be loud enough to be heard and determine a direction. And even if so, we are going to set a trap for them as soon as I get back."

When Toby returned with a rabbit and a sage hen, he found Julie sleeping soundly. He rummaged through the supplies he had abandoned after burying them in sand years ago, and found a tarnished, but usable pan, and another that had been used to boil water and make meat stew. He cleaned them with sand and water from the canteen he had filled from the spring below. Now all he needed was a fire.

He placed the rifle within quick reach, and broke dry pine sticks until he had a small pile of dry fuel. With considerable effort he got them flaming from a friction stick he carved with his knife. The small fire blazed with very little smoke. He was already frying the meat when Julie emerged from the cave. It was mid-morning.

Again Julie fearfully said, "Won't they see or smell the smoke?"

"Perhaps, but I really don't care."

"That doesn't sound like you. For heaven's sake, why not?"

Toby began unveiling his plan. "We've out run them as long as we can. They are bound to catch up with us soon, especially since we had to traverse the longer grass. I want whoever approaches to do so with the confidence that we are easy prey. And then we have to do this together."

"Toby, you know that I am up for anything."

"Yes, I know, but do you think you can accurately fire that rifle?"

"I'm sure I can. It's just like the one my Daddy used to have. He took me hunting many times. I shot my first deer when I was only nine, and many antelope and elk after that. I loved to shoot and was good at it."

"Fine! I am really glad to hear that! Now, look out there. We can see anyone approaching for almost two miles. I expect they are not searching together, so hopefully they will come one at a time. When we see a rider approach, I will sit out here on these rocks. He will surely ride his horse right up that ledge and stop within only a few feet from me. He'll believe I am helpless and an easy kill. But none of them will kill me before they locate you. That's certain. So with nothing to fear, they'll taunt me with threats and questions at close range. From the cave entrance, they should be an easy shot for you."

Julie gasped, "You want me to shoot whoever is after us? I'm not sure I can kill a human!"

"Don't think of them as a human. If they get their hands on you, you will not be treated humanely. It's self-defense, just plain survival. They can't let us survive, because our testimony will result in them going to the gallows. The only reason they spared us the first day was because of their greed. They hoped they could get even more money by ransoming us.

But you heard them. As soon as they got the money, they were going to bury us."

"Yes, I know. But it's still going to be very hard to shoot a living person. Why don't I stand out there as bait and you do the shooting?"

"No, emphatically no! Seeing you will make them cautious. They will suspect I may be hiding in ambush somewhere. More likely they would grab you and begin cutting until I appeared to save you, and you would be the shield preventing my shot. No Julie, that's too risky, and won't work. You will have to shoot one, and maybe even two men."

She sat, held her head in her hands and sobbed, "Oh God, how can I contemplate this? What gives me the right to end a human life?"

Toby continued his explanation. "Julie, when the time comes, it will not be that difficult. Take aim but do not fire until you see him move to his rifle, or raise it toward me. If possible, I will get him to brag about the train robbery and learn who has the gold, and where it is. But the moment he goes for the rifle, that's when you fire. And I need not tell you that it must be a kill shot. When you see right in your sights that he is going to kill me, I should hope it will come natural."

"It will not be natural. I can't even pray for strength, because I would be praying to kill a man."

"Julie, you know God prefers good over evil. When you see and hear this man again, you will not find it difficult to rise up to his evilness, and end it. You don't need to pray for strength."

"What about the ten commandments?"

"Look at it this way. If you don't act first, we will be zero broken while he breaks at least two. I think we will be forgiven."

She looked up, smiled and said, "Yes, you're probably right. Jesus loves you, but I'm his favorite." That was Julies shining personality, drawing humor from the depths of despair.

"OK pardner. We're together until, and even after 'Death do us part.'" After a moment of silence she asked, "Do you think they'll come at night?"

"No. Even with us unarmed, it would be too risky. They couldn't find their way up into these boulders in the dark. There will be almost no moon at all for the next couple of nights. We'll be OK tonight, but tomorrow may be the day."

Julie rubbed her forehead and said, "What do you say, let's eat."

Twenty-Four

Jim had no trouble following the trail north. Eddy's major concern was to avoid being ambushed from the rocks at the base of the ridges where Toby had wisely hidden many of their steps. Although Toby had done a good job hiding his trail, the bandits made no effort to hide theirs. His fear subsided when Jim confirmed that only one person was chasing their friends. One person would be concentrating on finding Toby and Julie, and less concerned about being sought themselves. He reasoned the two other gang members were fanned out to the east and west. It bothered him that the gang must have some rendezvous site where they would meet to evaluate their results. Riding up into such a meeting would not be good.

They made good time, pushing their animals constantly, and avoiding the diversions Toby had designed, because they could follow the rider ahead of them who wasted his time relocating the trail, but eventually got back on track.

By afternoon they could tell they had gained a day on the searcher before them, because they came upon his abandoned campsite. As Jim examined the site to assure there was still only one rider, three men on horseback appeared from over the east ridge. Jim watched them approach, and claimed he could tell by their dress and their ponies, they were Crow. He said, "Remember, we are still on the land of the Crow, and they hate the railroad."

Eddy climbed back on his horse, while Jim assumed a less threatening position standing near the burned fire pit. All three rode directly to them, a tactic not used if they meant immediate harm. Jim gestured that he would do the talking, and signaled a sign of peace to the arrivals. Eddy was content to oblige.

All of the discussion was done in the Crow language. Jim asked several questions, which provoked long answers. When Jim finally appeared to be providing answers or explanations to them, they became visibly angry, but apparently not at Jim. At the conclusion of the discussion, they turned and rode at a gallop in the direction from where they came.

Eddy asked, "What was that all about?"

"They met a man, not white, maybe Mexican, about an hour's ride from here. He was searching for a man and a woman who he said had stolen many cattle. He described them much like Toby and Julie; a 'fine looking woman with bright yellow hair.' The Mexican said the couple's horses were wild and ran from them, so now they walked. He asked for their help - said he would give them three ponies and much whiskey when they returned with both scalps."

"That's terrible. So what now?"

"I told them the man lied, and that he was bad. I made them know that the couple he sought were good people, friends of the Crow, and the reason the man wanted them dead was because they witnessed his bad deeds. I told them of the train robbery, and that the man and his white friends had stolen cattle from the Crow. They now know that we are looking for the same people to save them from the bad. I really angered them when I spoke that there would be no ponies and no whiskey, and that they were fooled. Their embarrassment will become shame unless they get revenge on the Mexican. I did not ask for their help. They are not good people themselves. They now ride to find the Mexican man again. I am sure it will be him that loses his scalp."

Eddy relieved, said, "Jim, you are great. I swear you are the smartest Crow on this great land. I sure am proud to be your friend."

Jim replied, "You have saved me many times from the white man's whip. My people are learning that we cannot escape to the old ways, and must make new ways work for us. You, my friends, are helping me learn to live with the changes. I now live good. You are a different white; my only blood brother."

They mounted and rode in silence. Eddy was certain the Mexican had sealed his fate and there would soon be only two remaining searchers working in the north, with possibly a third hunting nearer the river. Jim was uncertain about the numbers because he could not account for the four people who performed the train robbery. They were unaware of the demise of Kid. They still needed to be extremely cautious as they gained on what they believed to be the single bandit in pursuit.

Twenty-Five

It was almost perfectly dark, just what he wanted. Now he felt safe in forcing the railroad to comply with his demands. He cursed to himself, because he expected Sanchez to meet him near the Pompey's Pillar crossing, where they would travel a couple miles to the west and signal the late-night train with a green lantern. Sanchez didn't show up. The big man's anger was growing. He specifically told Sanchez to stay near the river camp, and only in the early mornings, travel north to meet Bolo who was searching to the northeast. Vincent was searching to the northwest. Bolo was to meet with Fred, at least every other day. He expected them to relay information to him by passing it on through each person. The big man had not heard from anyone in two days.

He muttered in the darkness, "I should have known not to trust a lazy drifter. The fool probably got lost, or fell off his horse someplace. Who knows where the other two are? Bolo is just about as unreliable as Sanchez."

Bossmiller, alone in the dark, with mental anguish, reviewed his gang's status. Bolo was older; an army deserter from the Civil War, twenty years ago. He got in a card game with Frank Vincent in Butte. Bolo caught Vincent cheating, but Frank was quicker on the draw, and would have killed Bolo except he still owed Frank money. They settled their dispute. Afterwards Vincent admired Bolo's toughness and cut him in on a couple of petty robberies, and later a bold stage robbery. In spite of their success, there was still bad blood between them.

The slow-moving freight train could be heard approaching from the west. The big man was also angry with himself because he did not specify which train, or from what direction the ransom bearing train should come from. He knew he doubled his risk by being trackside for any length of time. But who would find him along forty miles of track in the dark? In his mind, it was still a good plan. He waited until the train was in full view, lit the green glassed lantern, and waved it in a wide arc. The train did not slow down, and no package was thrown out. He searched the opposite side of the track on the chance they were unable to throw it at the lantern as instructed. Nothing.

It would be another hour before the next freight passed. He dared not wait in the same location. Moving steadily, he was three miles to the west, when he saw the light of the approaching steam engine. A green light was again swinging in an arc at trackside when the big engine passed. A second time, the train left nothing but smoke and ashes.

"Big B", as he was sometimes called, tried again the following night. Once more he was alone to perform his dark deed. This time he began earlier, and continued throughout the night, flagging three trains. He collected nothing, and shortly before dawn, rode toward the Pompey's river crossing.

He was furious. He knew the only person he could rely on was Vincent, although he did not trust him. Vincent was reliable only because he planned on splitting everything gained, only two ways, of course giving himself half. He knew, given the chance, Vincent would murder him along with the others he planned to disenfranchise in the same manner. But he too could cancel out Vincent. The known possibilities left them with a mutual working relationship.

He was at a loss to understand why Vincent had not returned with the railroad couple. They could not have outrun Vincent, they were on foot, and he was on a horse. In that blistering heat and wilderness they should be near dead in three days. If anyone could find them, it would be Vincent. But where was he? The railroad was not paying, and he needed to have both the captives in custody. His next plan was to cut the girls hair, and send it along with a finger of Toby's to the NP. That would surely get them to produce a money package.

But now he must find out what went wrong with the original plan. The river had receded. The boat was hidden in the willows. He would row across keeping the horse on a rope, swimming beside him.

Safely across, he rode into the north side river camp cautiously, but found none of his men were present. The camp looked abandoned. He had ordered Sanchez to maintain the camp. Sanchez did not know where the captured gold was hidden, leaving Big B more curious than concerned. It was not logical for him to leave without payment.

He tied his horse to a sage and walked toward the river. He sat in the shade of the nearest cottonwood to study the numerous footprints converging near the tree. He felt unusually uncomfortable, as if someone was watching him. He scanned the brush around him, with a strange feeling he was not alone. A small circle of dark red on the grass near his foot caused his eyes to rise. As he looked up, he was shocked by the horror scene above him. A few feet above his hat, he saw a hand and arm drooping from the tree. As he adjusted his eyes to the gruesome scene, he saw that Sanchez had been hung by his feet from a large overhanging branch. His body and arms dangled lifelessly upside down. He was suspended out of reach, making it impossible for Bossmiller to cut him down, and the big man, unlike the killers was unable to climb the tree. Missing were Sanchez's horse, his boots, and his scalp.

The gang leader, now feeling quite alone, knew this was not the work of Vincent or Bolo. He quickly retreated from the tree, and stood shaking by his horse. Completely unnerved, he reconsidered the abilities of Vincent. He too would be suffering in the parched wilderness to the north. He should have returned to camp by now. All were expecting to locate the runaways in short order, and none of the men were well equipped. The condition of Sanchez struck fear deep into Bossmiller. At first, he considered joining in the search, but the heat and terrain were not something he was accustomed to.

Now he began to think his entire gang may have been killed by a rogue band of Indians. None were his personal friends, and their demise would only increase his fortunes. The big man was in no mood to investigate further. Induced by fear, he recrossed the Yellowstone and rode to his temporary shelter to the east.

With the image of Sanchez suspended from the tree still in his mind, he decided to abandon the ransom effort. If Vincent survived, he would know how to get in contact at their home base miles from the Yellowstone. His major regret was that he could not bring all of the gold with him. The consoling factor was that Vincent didn't know where he had moved it.

Twenty-Six

Both Toby and Julie slept fitfully during the night; partly because they were used to traveling in the dark and sleeping in the daylight, but for the greater reason, they anticipated being found by potential killers in the morrow. Both understood the damage being done by the stress in which they were existing. Mental and physical exhaustion were robbing them of strength, but not their will to live. They continued to work together as loving partners. Both retained their faith that they would emerge victors.

When they woke, neither, even in their still hungry state could eat the meat Toby grilled. The morning air hung heavy on the rocky bluff, while Toby stood watch over the waving grass plain stretching out from their rocky perch above.

Toby felt no need to go over or rehearse the plan they had made. He would be the decoy. Julie would be the shooter.

An hour passed while Toby squinted into the distance. Julie fidgeted near the cave opening after repeatedly checking her view of Toby through her cover of low pine branches. She would lay, prone on her stomach, sight at the edge of a branch with the rifle barrel resting on the large rock in front of her.

She practiced getting into position, and experimented with her view. She believed it should be a steady shot with solid support for the rifle. Toby had checked the gun several times. It was loaded and ready to fire. Neither spoke, until finally Toby announced, "I see a rider coming."

The rider advanced steadily. The sun was at his back. He could see their rocky bluff in the sunlight, and spotted the game trail winding to the level where his victims were waiting. Toby picked up a snare he was mending, and gave the appearance he was concentrating on the task now resting in his lap. The rider rode confidently, making no attempt at stealth. Like a black death plague he moved steadily toward his sufferers. He was now close enough to be recognized. Scar-neck had found them.

He boldly rode his horse up the dead-end path, stopping only ten paces in front of Toby; a perfect set up for the shot from ten feet above him. With nerves of steel, Toby sat on the rock and stared at his long-time enemy. Scar-neck said nothing, staring back with an evil grin.

Toby broke the silence with, "Good morning Vincent. What took you so long?"

"You were pretty good with your night time tricks. But I knew I would wear you and your pretty friend down", he said with a raspy voice.

"I didn't think you would be the one to come after us. I thought you would be smarter than to traipse this far north and leave your thieving friends back there to run off with all that gold."

Scar-neck laughed, "It don't work that way. It's gonna be a two-way split when we get done. Plus the railroad's gonna give us a bonus for entertaining you for all this time. And I been wait'n five years to get even with you for our little tussle over there in Coulson."

Toby's mind was racing. He needed to get more information before Scar-neck made his move, but so far, his approach wasn't working. He tried again, "So where is your fat friend, Bossmiller? I can't believe you left him to split the gold; two pieces for him, one for you."

"By now, he's probably count'n more than gold. The railroad's gonna pay ten thousand apiece for you two highbrow buffalo chips. We got a foolproof way of gittin' the money, and they got no way of gittin' you. Now where's your pretty friend?"

Toby dropped his head for the first time, and looked at the ground. "She didn't make it. I left her back in the valley."

"That's a damn lie. There wasn't no grave back there, and you didn't even have a shovel to make one. Now, where is she?"

"I scraped out a shallow one and covered her with rocks. She got bit by a rattler."

"You're a lousy liar. She's hide'n round here someplace, probably shaking in her fancy bloomers, hoping you will talk me into leaving. She's a wild one. I'm still laugh'n 'bout when she knocked Kid on his ass. She's gonna be a lot of fun."

When Scar-neck used the word leave, it gave Toby another idea. "So you came up here to kill us.

That could be a big mistake. Why don't you ride off and just be a train robber, instead of a killer? They don't always hang robbers, but killing is sure to get your neck stretched."

"With you two dead, there ain't nobody else to tell who did it."

"What makes you so sure? How about your sister in Spokane? Maybe even the other three that were in on the robbery. Where are they?"

"You know, your talk'n is just convincing me that you know way more than you should. So I am going to carve it out of you, as to where Goldilocks is hiding. When I'm through with you that girly and me are going to have a two-day party. When I get tired of it, I'm gonna leave her carcass to rot in the sun, right alongside of yours. "

Uttering his last statement, Scar-neck did the unthinkable. He dismounted from his horse on its left, and drew a large skinning knife from his side. Now he stood with the horse between him and Julie. She could barely see his head above the horse's back, and as he advanced toward Toby, the horse covered him completely. She continued to lay prone, breathing deep with her hand tightening on the trigger. But she couldn't see her target.

The dismount caught Toby by surprise. He thought of going for his own knife in his boot, but the villain's advance was so quick he dared not take his eyes off him, or reach for anything. He came at Toby with the knife held high in one hand intending to slice it along Toby's torso.

Scar-neck interpreted Toby's good manners and business clothing as an indication of a soft "city slicker." It was a foolish mistake.

Toby jumped to his feet and immediately had his big hands around Scar-neck's knife bearing wrist. But that left the assailant with a free arm to strike Toby's face. The blow glanced to the side, throwing Scar-neck off balance. Toby swung a leg behind the wiry man and tripped him to the ground, while both were still grasping the long knife. Toby landed slightly downhill, giving Scar-neck the advantage of rolling on top of Toby. He pressed the knife toward Toby's chest with both hands, while Toby used his strength to hold it back and push Scar-neck off his chest. The weight and force of the robber was nearly equal to Toby's strength. The point of the knife in Scar-necks quivering wrist was beginning to penetrate Toby's shirt, and tattoo his chest with shallow cuts.

Julie, laying prone next to the rock could only see the battle through the legs of the horse. The two fighting on the ground were moving rapidly and too close together for her to get a clean shot. Now, lying prone, she was too close to the ground. The rolling struggle on the hillside put several large rocks in the path of an intended bullet. She abandoned her position, stood upright, and placed the rifle to her shoulder. Still, she could not shoot at the entwined, scuffling, twisting wrestlers.

Toby worked one leg from under Scar-neck and jerked his knee up to hit the knife supporting elbow. The knife lurched up across Toby's ear;

fortunately with the dull side as the leading edge, cutting nothing. Toby rolled out from under his burden and quickly rose to his feet. Scar-neck was slower, allowing Toby to land a foot on his chest, knocking him back over a knee-high rock. As Scar-neck regained his footing, Toby took the brief opportunity to bring his own knife from his boot. The knife, although much shorter than Scar-neck's, took away the advantage of the villain, and he clearly recognized it. He stood up and stepped back to his horse's side. With the horse still between himself and Julie's position, he drew his rifle from the scabbard.

Toby quickly moved to his left, crossing in front of the horse, moving into Julie's sights. He briefly saw Julie standing above him, rifle at the ready position. Scar-neck, preparing to shoot Toby, did not look above him. Toby moved around the horse's head toward the flank. Scar-neck followed, passed in front of the horse, and raised his rifle toward Toby.

Julie's rifle cracked, and a bullet struck Scar-neck in the shoulder, stopping somewhere in his chest. The penetrating shock spun him around. With his head thrown back, he saw her above him. Only one hand held his rifle, uncontrolled. He wildly pulled the trigger, discharging a bullet that struck the side of the cave opening, only inches from where Julie had been lying. She stood her ground, lowering the rifle only enough to quickly lever in another cartridge. A second report burst from Julie's rifle. The bullet entered Scar-neck's skull just above his right eye, and exited out the back of his neck. He fell at his horse's feet.

Toby caught one rein of the horse as he bolted away from the rifle shots. He quieted the animal, tied it to a tree branch and stumbled to a rock where he glanced at his bleeding chest. The cuts were only surface punctures and he quickly scrambled up to Julie who had fallen to the ground. Fearing she had been injured by the errant rifle shot, he carefully put his arm around her convulsing body. She was sobbing uncontrollably.

"Where are you hurt?", he asked.

"I'm OK", she said, but continued sobbing.

"It's alright, we had to do it", Toby consoled.

She replied in uncontrolled sobs, "No that's not it. I was glad to shoot him. But Toby, it's the gun. That's my Daddy's gun. How did you get my Daddy's gun? I killed a man with my Daddy's gun", she continued crying, barely able to talk.

Toby took the gun from her hands and looked at it closely. It was model 1866 Winchester .44 caliber lever action rifle. It was already known as the gun that won the west. It had been well used, and carried individual markings.

"Julie, life handed me an experience that I have never shared with anyone. We now have participated equally in life changing events. Let me hold you close, while I share my deepest secret."

He paused to arrange his thoughts around this never revealed event. "First, how are you sure that this is your Daddy's rifle?"

"I never had time to really look at it until after I shot this man. It felt so much like the one Daddy gave me to hunt with that I looked at it closely. There are marks that I put near the trigger guard every time I killed a large animal. There are five little marks on it I put there myself. This is my Daddy's gun that he stored in a rack over the barn door. I know it is his. One day he said it was missing, and speculated that one of the cowboys working for us may have borrowed it. But it was never returned. This is my Daddy's gun. How did you get it?"

Toby slowly and calmly told her the story, while he hugged her close patting and rubbing her shoulder. "I'm sure you remember Mean Morgan, who used to work for your father. He was rounding up stray cattle and found me here in this cave. I had no idea what had happened after you disappeared, but when Morgan confronted me, I saw the blue neck scarf you often wore, around his neck. I accused him of being responsible for your disappearance and he said he was going to kill me to keep me quiet. He was going to shoot me. We struggled in the cave, he was winning, but the wolf took him down, and I crushed his skull with a large rock. I buried him under a rock slide I created, just a few paces to the west of here. When I left, I buried everything of his, and whatever else I couldn't take with me. I saved the gun, wrapped it in canvas from our wrecked wagon and hid it in the sand. Somehow, I thought I might someday need to produce it to justify what I had done. When our lives were threatened out here, I brought us back to this gun, thinking it was the only thing we could use to keep us alive."

Calmed now, Julie spoke in deep reflection. "It's like the rainbow. It gave me strength, showing light and strength anchored with both ends in the rocks. My Daddy's gun gave me strength. I didn't just kill a man all by myself. My Daddy and this gun were with me. He saw me through this. He saved me and you too. She raised her head and looked at the thin clouds above. She breathed deeply, interrupted by a little hiccup sob and said, "Toby, I am going to be alright. I believe that killing a person will forever change us inside, but we must grow beyond it. We will be forgiven if we can forgive ourselves. How is your chest? Your shirt is cut and blood is soaking through."

She tore off a piece of her blouse, from the only clean portion that remained tucked into her skirt. She soaked it with clean water and scrubbed his wounds. A few punctures contained sand from rolling on the ground, but they had already stopped bleeding. Satisfied that cleaning was all she could do, she discarded the torn bottom of her blouse and said, "OK, let's bury this bastard."

It was the first time he had ever heard her curse; she used the word they had learned together years ago.

Toby guided her to the edge of the ravine west of the cave. They examined the boulders at the precipice and found plenty of loose giants poised to roll down into the gully. They returned to the lifeless body of the man who less than an hour ago was intent on killing them. Toby said to Julie, "You don't have to help me, I can do this alone."

She said, "No! I want to do this. After I again heard the horror of his plans, I killed him with no regrets. I still have no regrets, and I am going to enjoy seeing him covered with the biggest rock slide we can create."

She reached down, grabbed one of Scar-neck's hands and said to Toby, "Come on pardner, let's finish this."

She was a little too eager, and Toby knew she was covering up her lingering feeling of guilt. He had felt the same, five years ago in these same boulders. He hoped it would end here, but he had strong feelings of doubt.

They drug him down into the gully, climbed to the top, and working together created a train sized rock slide. All that remained of Scar-neck was his rifle, and his horse that could carry them away from their sandstone sanctuary.

Toby took the horse down to the west side of the rock ridge. He staked the animal in tall grass, out of sight from anyone arriving from the east. He would water the animal from the east side spring, but only after dark.

The afternoon was spent calming their nerves and more planning. Julie said, "We still aren't free, are we?"

"No, there are still two, and possibly three out there looking for us. Bolo and Sanchez are still out there, and who knows where Bossmiller is. I doubt he will leave the Yellowstone. He's the boss and is too smart to expose himself to the dirty work. But we have to watch for the other two."

"How can we get to safety?"

"I'm sure that Eddy is out there somewhere too. Let's give it two more days here. I believe we are safe at night, and we can still see everything that comes our way. It's a risk, because Bolo may arrive first, but we're getting good at this. Nothing says we can't do it all over again."

Julie looked at him and shook her head as if to say, "Never again."

Twenty-Seven

It had been hard for Toby and Julie to travel at night. But the men seeking to destroy them had horses. Toby was not confident they wouldn't travel through the darkness, but felt certain they would not be able to find the cave with the absence of sunlight. Julie was less certain.

They slept fitfully. Julie woke often with frightening nightmares. In the early morning light, Toby tried to calm Julie's fears. Her terse reply was, "During our short marriage, I have spent many wonderful nights with you. But this was not one of them."

"Julie, if they come again, there can't be more than two of them. This time I will hide in the rocks, away from the cave entrance. With Vincent's rifle in my hands, we can split our firepower into two directions. They'll still not be expecting us to be armed. They won't have a chance."

"OK, I know it sounds so easy, but it's not. Something always goes wrong, like Vincent getting off his horse. I was up here paralyzed, unable to do anything. Does his gun have extra shells?"

"The tube is full and I found more in his saddle bags."

"Good, then you shoot first. I'll take out whoever is left a second afterward."

She paused, thinking like an army tactician. "What if they don't come together. If they're smart, one will be several paces behind the other."

"If that happens, I will wait until the first stops, and the one in the rear closes the gap. Curiosity will keep him from staying behind for long."

"Toby, when we were kids, we never played cowboys and Indians, or cops and robbers. I'm not looking forward to this. I'm so upset I feel nauseous."

"That's because back then, we had no idea there were such conflicts. It's certainly not a fun game, but it is one we must play. In this game, I must tell you that I am a poor sport and refuse to be a loser."

It was settled; the plan was made. They would rest, heal their wounds and wait.

Late in the day, as Toby gazed off over the valley below him, something claimed his attention. He saw movement, still too far away to define. As he watched, he saw two, maybe three objects. He rubbed his eyes and tried to focus on the movement. Most likely it was wild game, but he watched the objects move steadily to the north. When the movement stopped, the objects became smaller, and Toby realized it was two riders who just dismounted. They were leading a third animal. They continued to close the distance until he could see the two men. He hoped it would be Eddy and most likely Jim Little Bear.

For some reason, the two paused and seemed to turn again to the north. Toby remembered he had created a diversion at that particular spot before he crossed the valley. He scrambled into the cave, and demanded, "Quick, give me anything shiny. Try one of those pots, or a buckle or anything." He grabbed their only tin container and jumped to a tall rock in the sunshine. He tried to create a heliograph to project a flash visible to the riders. Neither object was large enough or shiny enough. The riders continued north.

Toby grabbed his knife and shouted to Julie. "Quick, come help. Stir those coals. Throw some wood on the fire pit." He was excitedly cutting green branches from the nearby pines. He threw the cuttings near the pit, and pulled clumps of grass from beside the rocks.

Julie sensing the urgency, worked with him, finally asking, "What are we doing?"

"I saw two riders and a mule. One rode a pony without a saddle. I'm sure it was Eddy and Jim. They took the diversion trail and are still going north. We have to signal them somehow, and all we have left to try is a smoke signal."

"Good heavens, everything in the valley will see the smoke. We'll be inviting trouble."

"Maybe so, but there is safety in numbers. We risk failure, but we are doomed if we don't try."

The fire was flaming high when Toby poured water on their only blanket. He piled all of the green boughs and grass onto the flames. The greenery nearly smothered the fire, but produced thick grey smoke.

"Hear, take two corners of this blanket and help me hold down this smoke."

"OK, now move with me, pull it to the side, and let the smoke puff up."

"Great, now let's cover it again and hold it down until the smoke starts coming out around the sides."

"That's good, now let it go again."

After creating three puffs of smoke that rose into the sky above their ridge, Toby pulled the burning branches and kicked the grass away from the fire. He managed to squelch the smoking debris and returned to his lookout rock, holding his newly possessed rifle. He looked back at Julie, and smiled.

"Good job", he said.

"I love a man who can smile into trouble", she said, wiping the sweat from her forehead.

Time passed at the speed of ancient glaciers. Finally a lone rider appeared, trailing a pack mule. It certainly resembled Eddy, but Toby was alarmed at the absence of the second rider.

Toby sat poised with the rifle on his knee. He saw Julie in the cave opening, holding her Winchester.

A familiar voice hit him with, "Hey Bub, you smoking a turkey?"

Julie exclaimed from above, "Oh, Eddy. Thank God it's you."

Toby still puzzled asked, "Where's Jim?"

Eddy glanced at Julie and said, "Look right there above her." As he spoke, he waved to the ledge above the cave, and the silent protector waved back and disappeared. He rode up a few minutes later.

Toby, still concerned for their safety asked, "How noticeable were the smoke signals."

"Barely visible. We were lucky to see them, but we were constantly looking around us. I knew we had to be close, but I was looking at what I thought was your third fake to the west, and wanted to explore to the north first."

Jim, displaying a rare sense of humor said, "Your smoke spelling is terrible."

Eddy looked at Julie, whom he hadn't seen in two years. She stood before him a raw beauty. He said, "You are beautiful as ever my dear." He might have gotten away with it, if he had not cracked an impish smile.

She glared at him, blue eyes flashing. Her once white blouse was, ripped at the shoulder, with the bottom torn completely off, and what remained was stained with dirt and dried blood. Her fashionable split riding skirt was shredded at the bottom with cheat grass seeds and sand burrs stuck in the material, the remnants hanging over her scuffed and dirty boots. A scab was still partly hanging from her chin, accompanied by healing sun blisters on her forehead, while mosquito bites dotted her cheeks. Her elbows were bruised and skinned from falling in the darkness. The famous golden hair, unbrushed or washed for a week, hung disheveled adorned by imbedded bits of grass and sage.

She politely said, "Eddy, if I would have known when you were coming, I would have put on a nicer dress.

Good natured ribbing drew chuckles from everyone. In a much-elevated mood all turned to the pack animal. The starving couple were soon overjoyed with a variety of food, cooking utensils, clean canteens and two clean bed rolls.

Julie went to work, making the evening meal, appearing overjoyed with the task. As a group they recounted their experiences. The stories soon wound themselves together.

Eddy was most interested in what happened to Scar-neck. Toby fibbed, interjecting, "I had to shoot him before he shot me." Julie stood up from her perch by the firepit and said, "Tobias Hawthorn, you don't have to cover for me. I shot Vincent, and given the chance, I'd do it again. I regret I only got to shoot him twice, because he had much worse planned for me. I hope he renders in the worst part of hell."

Eddy glanced at Toby, and tipped his hat at Julie in a cowboy salute. Jim, smiled and looked into the fire, speaking only with eyes of admiration.

They summarized: Scar-neck, Kid, and Sanchez were dead. Only Bolo was left to pursue them. Bossmiller, also called Bossman and Big B, was the true leader of the gang, and was probably the one who stayed behind, demanding the kidnap ransom. Angela Vincent Coulter was Scar-neck's sister, and their source of NP information. Toby was still not sure Angela was a willing participant. Julie believed she was a scheming partner to it all.

Toby drew an important conclusion. "We four are the only people that know most of the circumstances. Bossmiller must still think his participation is undiscovered. He does not know that Julie and I were hiding in the rocks above him the night he came to their camp. He's still out there with a stolen fortune, and in his mind still not suspected of anything. If he's still out there, Bolo is the only one left to tell Bossmiller anything.

Eddy said, "The NP offered a big reward for your recovery, and any information leading to the capture of the robbers. Would you guys mind if Jim and I collected that? I know that I still work for the NP, but heck, I'd quit to collect. It's going to be more money than we make in five years. I don't know how we'll prove the gang members are dead, but they will maybe just have to believe us."

Jim said, "I guess you should have taken scalps. I'm sure the Crow party will have taken Sanchez's"

Julie shuddered.

Toby said, "One way would be to capture Bossmiller. I'm sure there will be a reward for recovering the gold."

"Now boys, those sunbeams are still on the horizon. First we have to get out from under the storm around us." She handed out tin plates and served her first hostess dinner.

When it was dark, the horses were stashed on the west side, and all retired to the safety of the cave; four tired bodies, each lying within scant inches of four rifles.

Twenty-Eight

Before the sun broke over the hills, Jim was in the lead, Toby and Julie rode double on the horse once ridden by Vincent, and Eddy trailed, tethered to the pack mule. Jim kept close watch on the trail ahead while Eddy watched behind. All looked to the boulders and high points. They decided the safest route was to continue north. They would ride through the homestead now owned by Toby, and rest at what was now Julie's ranch, willed by her mother. The ranch was leased for cattle grazing, and the house, according to the lease agreement, was occupied by only a single hired hand. From there, they planned to return by passing through Roundup on their way to Billings. Hopes were that in Billings they could arrange with the NP to transport them and their horses back to Miles City. The northern route was traveled by many, including the stage. Toby had learned a railroad spur was even being built to service the area and the expanding coal mines. Both he and Julie longed to see the old homesteads. She asked Toby how far he thought they were from his homestead. His reply was, "About a day's ride."

They rode in silence. Julie was daydreaming of the home she left five years ago. She knew it would be changed, but she couldn't help thinking of how it had been to the little girl who still lived within her. It was a happy place. At least that is what she remembered. In her deep thoughts, she relived her fossil collecting expeditions. Alone with her little straw basket, she dug at the base of the clay bluffs only a quarter mile from her house. She loved finding skeletal remains of prehistoric creatures. She wandered the bluffs in solitude, imagining a life among the prehistoric creatures. There, in her secret places among the rocks, she absorbed the placidity and quietude into her soul and her ordered childhood life.

As she was recalling the joy of strolling among spring flowers, a rifle shot pierced the silence while at the same time, she saw a red mist erupt from the back of Jim's shirt. Ahead of her, she saw Jim lurch backward, then fall forward onto his saddle horn. His startled horse side stepped, causing Jim to tumble to his left, grab the horse's mane, and fall to the ground. Behind her, Toby yelled, "It's from up above. Get in the rocks!"

Toby reined their horse next to a pile of sandstone and pulled Julie down to the ground. A second shot rang out, then a third glanced off the rock above them. Toby tried to look up toward the shooter but the morning sun blazing above the rocks prevented him from seeing anything. Eddy cut loose the mule and rode to where Jim lay in the sage. He jumped from his saddle, grabbed Jim's arms and drug him to the safety of the large boulders. As Eddy retrieved his horse, at the same time pulling his rifle from the scabbard, another bullet split the air cutting a path across Eddy's pant leg, tearing the top of his boot. Eddy, unfazed, only glanced at his foot as if he had just tripped on a stick. He returned to the rocks but chose not to reveal his position by firing back. When they were all sheltered in the rocks, the shelling stopped.

Eddy rolled Jim onto his back and opened his shirt. The sight struck them all. A gaping hole was in his chest. Each breath caused a rush of blood from the hole. Eddy called for his companions to help. They were already there. Eddy tried compressing Jim's bandana onto the wound, but nothing could be done. Blocking the hole was of no value, because it did not slow the massive internal bleeding. Jim was barely conscious, and knew he was fatally wounded. He smiled peacefully and said, "The eagle flies alone. Now I will fly with him." Two more breaths, his eyes closed, a quick shudder and he lay still. Jim Little Bear had died a young man.

Eddie looked up at the ridge. "I'm going after him. He can't get off of there easily. Stay here, he may be looking for us to make a run to the north."

Toby said, "Eddie, don't go alone." But Eddie heard nothing. His blood brother had just been killed.

Before Toby could retrieve their rifles, Eddy was gone, whipping his horse up the bluffs toward the ridge top, rifle in hand. Julie put her hand on Toby's neck and whispered, "You can't stop him. Eddy will die for his friends. You know that. If he doesn't find Bolo, that single shot will have killed them both."

Toby moved them further into the rubble, where he and Julie could shoot in three directions. Neither could force themselves to glance at Jim who lay at the edge of the sandstone. There they sat and listened…to nothing. Not even the cold breeze of reality creeping down their necks stirred them from their position. They were trapped until Eddy returned. And if he did not return then Toby must follow his trail. He was thinking of the consequences when he heard a shot from above him; a pause and two more shots. Toby's hopes elevated, because he believed the second two sounded like Eddy's long rifle. Toby fiercely fought the urge to go to Eddy's side. But he could not leave Julie, and good reason dictated he should not bring two more targets to the shooter. They waited; huddled down for safety.

A shaggy coyote slinked his way toward them, beckoned by the smell of blood. Toby broke the stillness by tossing a rock in the coyote's direction. The wary animal retreated, but not beyond his range of senses. The coyote now waited with them. As Toby was about to throw another, the varmint bolted off into the brush. The coyote was running from an approaching rider, no, two riders, no, one rider with a second horse. Eddy had returned with the shooter's ride.

Eddy dismounted without saying anything. Julie embraced him with a quick hug, that he rudely brushed away. He said, "I brought you a horse. Bolo won't need it. The money in his saddle bags, I will take to Jim's mother."

They both knew not to ask any questions. Eddy would explain with the passage of time.

Eddy sat on the ground beside Jim. He touched Jim's stiffening hand and wept. Toby had never seen Eddy release that much emotion. It tore at his own soul. He took Julie by the arm, and walked tearfully to a distance where Eddy could be alone with Jim. It was the only thing they could do.

When they returned, Eddie had covered Jim with a blanket. He sat looking out at the setting sun.

"You two will be safe now. I won't be going with you. I am taking Jim back down into Crow Country. He must be buried on his own land. I cannot burn him in Indian tradition but I can lay him in the land of his people. I'll join you in Billings at the train depot five days from now."

Julie asked, "Surely you will wait until morning. The moon gives almost no light tonight."

"I will go first thing in the morning. Two horses with saddles should help you make good time going north. You take most of the supplies. Jim's pony will carry him. When I return Jim to his land, I will turn the pony loose to run with the wind, as he did when Jim found him."

The evening darkened. Where Julie lay at the base of the boulders, she could see Eddie had not retired. He sat next to Jim's lifeless body. Late into the night, she woke, to find Eddie silently maintaining his vigil. He would not leave his friend alone through the night. When she could no longer sleep, she rose, carrying an unused blanket to the sentinel, placing it over his shoulders. She sat beside him in the cool night air.

Eddy was Toby's friend. She had not the opportunity to get to know the real Eddy. He only appeared at times to be the energy at the party, or the rascal in the play. Like a nurse, willing to heal the sick, she offered to receive his thoughts. She softly asked, "Did you know him long?"

Eddy spoke in a far-off voice, "I met him in grade school, in a little town near Wyoming Territory. He was a Crow, but his mother was half white. She wanted him to go to a white school, to learn "the new ways." My Dad was a bootlegger. Neither of us fit in with the others, and we became good friends. It was worse for Jim. Kids would not let him forget he was Indian, and constantly harassed him. I fought by his side. I was strong for my age and got pretty good at it, so when we were together, they left him alone. But he got tired of being the outsider, so he left the school, and lived with the Crow people, but only for a short time. Because of his "white man ways", he didn't fit in there either. One afternoon, he came to the school. It was spring and I was just finishing the eighth grade. My Dad was an alcoholic, and beat me every time he got drunk. So Jim and I decided to run off. We stole a couple of horses and rode to Colorado. We almost died crossing Wyoming. At age fifteen, and hungry we were nearly starved by the time we found a ranch. An old fella there took us in and gave us a job breaking horses. That became our profession. We broke horses from Colorado all the way into Canada. We healed each other's wounds, shared our good fortunes and jointly suffered poverty. In Canada Jim met a girl. It was young love, but the girl's father was a preacher. He forbade her to befriend an Indian. The father sent the girl away and ran us off. Jim never had a girlfriend after that. Finally, we traveled to Coulson to help build the railroad. We couldn't get with the railroad right away, so we found work cutting firewood. That's where we met first you, and later Toby. Jim's people hated the railroad. He always stayed loyal to his people, so he changed his mind and turned his back on the NP. He went to gold mining in Virginia City. Once again, he became an Indian in a white man's world. He left there broke, and we joined back up in Miles City. He got a job in the sawmill…the worst job they had in the company. But he worked hard and they liked him.

Jim was a loyal friend of almost twenty years. With him I could think aloud. The most he ever wanted from me was to be his friend. He was the person who would walk in for you, when the rest of the world walked out. I was honored to walk with him, but now I am deeply saddened that I did."

Julie listened, emotionally moved. When Eddy paused, she said, "Eddy, I am so very sorry. I have no cure for your pain. The only thing I can offer is my understanding." In the background she heard Toby stir, and knew that he too was listening.

The stars began to fade as morning approached. Eddy, in spite of his all-night vigil was regaining his strength. His personal emotions still poured out onto Julie.

"Jim was introverted, but very wise, with great inner conviction. He once told me, 'If a man doesn't know what principles he would die for, he is not yet ready to live.' He often reminded me that the future comes one day at a time, and that I should begin each day planning to make my life better. He urged me to find stability and with it find love. Neither of us did so, though I had some opportunities. I told him I wasn't ready to change. He said we must change because it is the way of life. He said that if the world had no changes, we would not have butterflies. I think we both resisted the change because the emptiness without love, was something we shared. That kind of a change would have weakened our bond. But I know that he was right."

"Julie, as I look at you and Toby, I see so much that I have missed. Only in the last few weeks have I felt what it was like to be truly loved and needed. I have gone on many adventures without anyone despairing at my departure. There was rarely anything to return for. Jim, and a major part of my life, have in a heartbeat, been swept out of existence; turned into memories. He has pushed me forward. Now to make my dreams come true, I have to wake up."

With finality, he took a deep breath and said, "When I get back to Miles City, I am going to get married. Alice has subtly implied she wants to wed. Her nephew Timmy made it even plainer. When it happens, and it will be soon, I would like you and Toby to be there."

Julie was too choked up to speak. She hugged his shoulders and rose to dry her eyes.

Seeing that Eddy was preparing to leave, she put part of the remaining food into a saddle bag and placed it on Eddy's horse. "Here, take this with you. We won't need it all."

Eddy then took from the mule pack a rolled-up bundle of cloth, when unfolded became a man's shirt. Handing it to Julie, he said, "And you take this. You need it more than I do."

She blanched, dropping her hands to her side. "Is this Jim's shirt?"

"No it is not. It was to belong to the first one that needed it. There's Levi's in there too, but it looks like you're built different."

She was not offended. It was good to see Eddy fighting back his grief.

Toby, now fully awake after hearing most of the conversation, changed the subject with a probing question. "Eddy, I've been thinking how crazy it was for Bolo to take on four of us with so little planning. Had he prepared an ambush for whoever came after him?"

Eddy was preparing to drape Jim over his pony, which neither Julie or Toby wanted to see. But he stopped and explained, "There's more that you need to know. I think he wanted to die."

In disbelief Toby said, "What?"

Eddy continued, "When I rode up on him, I will have to admit that I was in a careless rage. I saw him clearly exposed and realized I too was an easy target. I jumped to the ground and fell prone to make as small a target as possible, but I was right out in the open. He stood upright at the side of a rock that he could have easily used for cover, and fired one shot at me. He missed by an arm's length. I shot twice, both striking his chest. He fell forward, but when I went to him, I saw old blood around a still bleeding hole in his back. Bolo was already a dying man because someone shot him in the back, and probably left him for dead. I think he wanted us to put him out of his misery, and he, for no real reason picked Jim to start the process."

Toby thought not long, before he said to Julie, "Do you remember what Scar-neck said when he was confident he was going to eliminate me?"

"Yes, he said that when all of this was done, the money would be divided with a two-way split."

"Exactly!", Toby exclaimed. "I thought that was strange at the time, but his big skinning knife kept me from asking for any details. Do you suppose Scar-neck knew he had us located, and figured he didn't need Bolo anymore? So he shot him in the back to reduce the number sharing the loot. He probably planned on killing Sanchez too, but Jim engineered that job for him."

Eddy said, "That's what it looks like. It's something Scar-neck would do. Now all that's left is Bossmiller. The way I look at it, he's now money in the bank. But I've got things to do first."

He wrapped Jim in his bedroll and tied him to the pony. He said a quiet goodbye, leading the pony off at a slow walk, saying over his shoulder, "I'll see you in Billings at the Depot."

Once again, they were alone.

Twenty-Nine

Two horses and a mule walked north. The couple rode in silence, until the sun appeared in full.

Julie asked, "Did you know him well?"

Toby answered. "I liked him very much, but he was hard to get to know. You only learned about Jim by being around him. He never handed you his thoughts. They sort of had to rub off on you."

"That's what I thought too. It's terrible when someone you know becomes someone you knew."

Toby said, "Life is usually pleasant. Death becomes peaceful. But the transition is awful."

Sunshine quietly rose the temperature around them until Julie asked, "Toby is there a creek anywhere near us? If so, I want to go there, even if it is just a little puddle."

"OK, let me guess why."

"You know darn good and well why. I am so dirty I am surprised this horse doesn't buck me off. She smells better than I do. I want to bathe and wash my hair. When I feel human again, I'll put on this men's shirt and smack anyone who offers one snide remark."

"I'm not sure, but I think there is a small stream about an hour ahead. It's been a long time since I hunted this area with my Pa, and I really don't remember. There's one up by our old homestead, but that's several hours away. Maybe I should just pray for rain."

"Then you better pray for thunder and lightning too, because it will be nothing like the storm I will create if I don't get to wash this cursed journey off me soon."

Toby laughed and said, "Come on horse, find water. I can't stand lightening when it's close."

A pine tree line in the distance gave hope. Toby nudged his horse at the site of possible water, causing the mule to rebel under his pack. Over his objections, they were soon at the rocky creek that appeared to be wringing the last rivulets of water from the now absent spring rains.

As soon as Julie's feet hit the ground, she became camp commander. "Here, tie up this mare, while I see what else is in that mule pack."

Eddy, an unusually clean cowboy had included a small wrapper of lye soap. She hung her ragged clothes on pine branches and sat in the stream pebbles. She washed, scrubbed, rinsed and repeated it all over again.

Toby, watching intently, both the scene before him and the horizon for riders asked, "Isn't that cold?"

"Yes, it's really cold, but it hurts so good. You know, you should really come in too."

"I would, but there isn't room in that little creek for both of us. I'll wait until you're done.

Besides, I like the view from here and I don't want to miss anything."

She got up, shook herself dry, and mooned him in the process.

"Chicken," she said. "Why don't you get in with your clothes on, and give them a wash too. Or on second thought, why don't you take your clothes off, bathe and then wash your clothes. I'll stand watch so that the magpies don't run away with any worms." She laughed heartily at her own joke.

Toby marveled at her ability to turn her face to the sunshine and leave the shadows behind her.

At her insistence, all of their clothing was washed and hung on the prideful pine that could have blushed with its trimmings. Sunshine and soft breezes soon dried the garments which were again adorned to prevent sunburn.

As they mounted up, Toby said, "I think we are about two hours from the old homestead."

The newlyweds now rode through the valley, with the shadow of death brushed into the past.

"I remember one thing that Jim said a long time ago. He said it was a Crow belief. The lesson was, 'Give thanks for unknown blessings already on their way.' Jim treasured things he learned from his elders."

Julie said, "That's uplifting, we could use a turn of good luck."

They rode until the site of the old dugout, Toby's childhood home, came into view. He stopped in the shade of the creek's border of trees. Beside him the original gravestone rested over his mother. He bent over and pulled a few long blades of grass from the rough edges. He viewed the humble marker with tears swelling in his eyes. It was still a peaceful scene. The roof of the old shelter had long given up holding the earth above it. It was now a pile of dirt and rotted wood leaning against a sandstone wall. Tall grass revealed no trespassers had recently explored the ruins.

Toby peeked through the rubble at whatever remained of the contents, while Julie remained mounted. Someone had removed the iron stove. A few old tin cans and bits of oil cloth were all that revealed humans had once lived and loved there. Only a few corral posts remained, their adjoining rails weathered and broken. He looked for signs of his past existence, but found none.

Visibly disturbed, Toby returned back to his ride and commented, "It's not quite as I remembered." In an emotional voice he said, "Let's be off, I've left nothing here."

But as they departed, he lovingly drank in the sights he once lived among; the picturesque creek, the rolling grassland and the long-needled pines. Memories transformed it into a place one could still call home. The land he still owned was open-range grassland. He wasn't even sure where he would find the boundaries.

Thirty

It was a nine-mile ride to Julie's ranch. She too, had not seen her old home for over five years. When her father died, her mother placed it into the care of a territorial bank who leased the land. When they were within a mile of the ranch house, her heart beat accelerated in fear and anticipation. She feared she would find a mess similar to Toby's old shelter, and yet excitedly anticipated being "Home."

They tied their horses near the front porch. Julie knocked on the front door. An old cowboy came to greet her, saying, "You must be lost."

Julie said, "And you must be the caretaker here. My name is Julie Hawthorn." She smiled because it was the first time she had ever uttered those words. She quickly realized from the old boy's expression, that the name meant nothing to him. She followed up with, "I am the owner of this ranch."

The announcement caught the caretaker by surprise, and he uttered a long, "No-o-o."

"I'm sorry. Let me explain. My mother was Mary Carlson. After my father died, she leased this ranch to whomever you work for."

The old man brightened up. "Oh sure. I knew your folks, great people; sure was a bad deal, your dad gittin' kilt by that devil horse. And I guess your mom died just a few months ago."

The watery eyed old fellow put a shaky hand on the door latch and said, "What can I do for you?"

Julie dripped the charm into her voice, "I realize this is where you live at this time, but I haven't seen this place in five years. Could I possibly come in and look around?"

"Oh yes mam. You and your friend there can come on in."

Julie introduced Toby as her husband. The caretaker put forth his calloused hand saying, "I'm Lem Kettelson. Glad to meetcha."

Julie was shocked to see the house was almost as she left it. However it appeared untouched by a housekeeper. Her mother's frilly curtains remained, but sagged under fly specks and inattention. Cracks in the floor boards were filled with dirt. Windows, still sound were now opaque. The fireplace overflowed with ash. It appeared only one bedroom had been used; two others hosted only multitudes of cobwebs.

In spite of the unkept house, Julie was pleased to see the still solid log building in good repairable condition. Lem offered them coffee, but Julie declined, thinking the cups probably had not been washed any more often than the floor.

After the coffee was declined, the old cowboy looked directly at Julie and asked, "I figure you are looking at the place wondering whether you should move back here and work it?"

Julie paused, searching for an indirect answer.

Lem took a step closer to her and slowly said, "Honey, when yer a holdin a lemon in your hand, ya have ta figure out if the juice is worth the squeezing." After speaking he sighed, turned, and put an empty cup back onto the kitchen shelf.

Julie did not reply, but her eyes narrowed until little wrinkles were visible above her cheeks, while she unconsciously chewed her jaw. She politely excused herself, allowing Toby and her to move outside and examine the barns and cattle pens. She was pleased to see they were in much better condition. Repairs and additions were made in good form, obviously by someone other than Lem.

Satisfied with her inspection, Julie did not linger in the nostalgia of her childhood playground. She and Toby rode north again, to their campground for the night.

Settled around the circle of rocks containing their fire, Toby asked, "Well, what do you think?"

"I've just now began to think. I had to get away from the place to clear my mind. The home is still very livable, but if it continues to suffer from the lack of care, it will soon become a dust pile. The working part of the place is still quite functional. But I am at a loss as what to do with it."

"What does your heart tell you to do with it?"

"My heart has been through such a gauntlet this last month, it's begging for a rest. I realize that you can never go back. You can't relive what you remember, or delve into moldy old thoughts for long. But it's even more beautiful out here than I remembered. As a child I took it for granted, because

I knew nothing else. But the real world we came from, the city, has trapped me into simple tiresome repetitions of life. What is their value? Did God create all of this for me to ignore? Am I wrong in thinking you perceive our existence as I do? Up until recently, we were both forced to accept what life had thrown us. When we were back there hiding in the rocks, not knowing if we were going to live another day, I made a promise for both of us. If I was ever given the chance, I vowed to grasp the end of that rainbow and create a life as vibrant as the colors within. I'm now holding that chance in my hand, and I must decide what I, no we, are going to do with it. Toby, I feel we need to live together for a while before we decide."

They both sat silently until Toby had digested all of her response. "My heart beats with yours. I won't be happy, if I continue running errands for bloated egos within the NP. However when I surveyed what was left of my parent's lives, I saw nothing. The land is as vacant as they found it. My plague is the fear of losing the security that the NP offers. But my mind has been exploring the possibilities of a myriad of other ventures."

Julie offered, "In addition to this place of my parents', Aunt Rosie has left me her home and a small fortune, which could purchase every bit of land between your boundary and mine. But we would be buying our way into a lifetime of hard work."

Toby stroked her long braids and concluded. "I agree. Let's contemplate these decisions through a couple of seasons until we can follow that rainbow with confidence. The ranch will keep until then."

For the first time in days, they slept in peace.

Thirty-One

The next morning they continued north until they came to the Musselshell river and the small settlement of Musselshell. Julie saw and remembered the site north of the river called Musselshell crossing, where herds of Texas longhorns were driven from the south and were held until they were broken up into smaller groups and spread out to their new Montana owners. Her father had purchased cattle there. She was pleasantly surprised to find the little store on the opposite side was well stocked and now contained a post office. She was amused to think her parents' old homestead was now less than an hour ride from a post office. At Musselshell they turned left to the west, bound for Roundup.

In Roundup, Julie learned that all territorial papers concerning land and deeds were stored in the judicial court system in Helena. Mr. Lavine, Toby's barrister friend, would have to deal with the recording and legal processes.

The ride from the Musselshell to Coulson and Billings, took three days, mainly because they were still dragging the mule. The animal was tolerated, because he allowed them to travel in relative comfort, thanks to the supplies Eddy had provided.

Both Toby and Julie were concerned about the very hot weather. Not just because it was unpleasant traveling in the heat, but because the normally green hillsides were already turning brown. Grass was no longer growing, and range feed would be scarce in the coming winter. Not many settlers in the area grew crops, but those who did, would surely reap little to nothing. The prevailing weather was also an important consideration in deciding what to do with their Musselshell property.

As soon as they arrived in Billings, Julie became self-conscious about her disheveled appearance. They had one day to recuperate before meeting Eddy at the train Depot. Toby too felt he should improve his current form, although he reminisced about how much better it was than his initial condition in Coulson at age fifteen. They had been thrifty with their traveling money, and a few Billings merchants remembered Toby from his NP employment in the area. With the combination, they were able to gain enough good faith credit to "reoutfit" themselves, although their purchases were much more practical than they were fashionable. Baths in a clean hotel after supper raised their spirits and prepared them for tomorrow.

Eddy met them in the Billings train depot at noon. He already completed arrangements to transport their livestock in a freight train leaving in the mid-afternoon. The preparations included a free ride in the caboose for all of them. He financed his evening in town by selling the rifle that once belonged to Bolo. He still traveled with two long guns, his own and Jim's, now his most precious.

The trio was exhausted from their previous ordeal, and spoke little until they arrived in Miles City. Eddy pleased both of his friends by presenting them with their personal effects that were abandoned on the train as a result of their capture.

Eddy said, "You are welcome to spend the evening in my humble shack. It's big enough for three. But I suggest we pay a surprise visit to my friend Alice. She will be happy to see us."

Eddy was a kidder, but not a fool. He sent a telegram to Alice the evening before, warning of their return. He was sure they would be welcomed.

Eddy's homecoming was so overwhelming he was embarrassed. Timmy was uncontrollably happy to see Eddy return. But the evening did not advance without the discussion turning toward their future plans. Eddy was determined that he would collect the reward for recovering Julie and Toby, and all agreed. He was additionally motivated to find and present Bossmiller to authorities, and ultimately collect for locating the stolen loot. Eddy was clearly not planning a future with the NP and saw his chance to obtain a "grubstake". They resolved to disclose all information necessary to confirm Bossmiller was responsible for everything, to include the cattle shipping fraud, to the train robbery and to kidnapping. However, they agreed to withhold information about his suspected location and the possibility that Angela, in Spokane, may be involved in the entire scheme. After several hours of discussion, they developed a plan.

Toby would convince Mr. Hanson at NP headquarters, that he and Julie should pursue the truth concerning Angela and the cattle shipping fraud. Julie's presence was recommended to provide assistance in gaining Angela's cooperation. Intentions were, they would pressure her into giving information about her brother Vincent, and possibly Bossmiller, who perhaps was still residing in Spokane. Eddy would collect on the kidnapping reward, even if it meant he had to resign from the NP. In addition, he would obtain a leave of absence to hunt down Bossmiller. Again, if the temporary release was denied, he would resign until he was successful. Contact would be maintained by telegram, until they were able to join together to hunt Bossmiller. Eddy would begin by searching the banks of the Yellowstone east of the Pompey's river crossing, the last known presence of the gold. They would tap into the NP for Toby and Julie's transportation and expenses, while Eddy would use the money from the first reward.

Alice insisted that Toby and Julie spend the night in her extra bedroom. They retired to leave Eddy and Alice with time alone. Both remembered that Eddy said he planned to be married soon. Toby said, "I wonder if that will be before, or after he finds Bossmiller."

Toby left the house early the next morning, leaving Alice and Julie imbibing in tea and ladies talk. He spent the entire morning trading telegrams with

Mr. Hanson in St. Paul. In the end, the supervising gentleman was quite generous and understanding. He agreed to finance their expedition because of his confidence in all of them, but even more so because they were less expensive than employing the Pinkerton Company. The negotiation for the rewards was more difficult. The amounts had to be coordinated and agreed upon by top management, and the brokers involved in the gold shipment. The final terms were: Eddy would collect ten thousand, which had already been advertised, for *Information and the location of two NP employees, specifically, Toby and Julie;* a separate reward of ten thousand would be offered for information leading to the *location or apprehension of (first name unknown) Bossmiller, also known as Bossman and Big B*; and a third reward of twenty thousand was offered by the entities owning the gold for *information leading to the recovery of mineral assets unlawfully obtained from the NP railroad while in transit.*

Toby argued that the reward for the gold recovery should be larger because of the much greater value of the precious metal. However that reward was beyond the control of the NP. Toby was quite satisfied with the prospect of an additional thirty thousand for finding Bossmiller and his loot. Eddy was more than pleased. He was promised his money within the next five days.

After another conference, they agreed to begin their search immediately. Toby and Julie would board the next passenger train to Spokane. Eddy would start his search of the Yellowstone by embarking at the

Pompey's crossing and working east. Because the robbers used a boat, it would involve searching both sides of the river. He hoped to find an abandoned boat, another camp, or a place gold could be stashed. Somehow, Bossmiller transported a heavy load from the riverside a considerable distance, or stashed it nearby until it was safe to operate openly, perhaps with the prospect of Scar-neck's help. Eddy would replenish the mule pack and leave the next day.

Although Eddy did not mention it, Alice confided in Julie, that Eddy had proposed. She was overjoyed, but once again very concerned about another dangerous escapade. She revealed her mature understanding of Eddy by telling Julie, "Eddy is a very independent person who has survived living on the threshold of life and death. The loss of his friend Jim has distressed him greatly, and caused him to realize that life is not infinite. I'm sure he will seek revenge, which I hope will be somewhat mitigated by the reward money. But no amount of money will ever replace his friend, and one way or another, Mr. Bossmiller will pay dearly.

Eddy loves us but is too proud to bind me into a marriage without the means to give me a proper home. He sees this as an opportunity to begin a new life, and he will risk his own to do so. I love him so I must free him to slay his dragon. In his current state of mind, he will ride to the end of the earth to make it happen.."

Thirty-Two

Two days later, Toby and Julie stepped off the train in Spokane. The journey was not as luxurious as it was during their June ride, but employees still rode in comfort. A plan was developed while they were crossing the mountains. After consulting with the Spokane superintendent, they would remove Angela from her office and question her. Toby would be forceful, while Julie would be sympathetic. After an appropriate time, Toby would leave the two women alone to allow Julie to use her charm. He would privately question Vera, the assistant, to learn what she might say about the gold shipment.

The helpful superintendent provided a private room in which to perform their questioning. Angela Vincent Coulter was summoned to the waiting pair. She appeared much as before, tired, dispirited and apprehensive. Toby began with a friendly introduction.

"Angela, this is Julie Hawthorn, also an employee of the NP. We're here to expand our investigation of the livestock inventory irregularities. I'm going to get right to the point. We've learned that your brother, Fred Vincent, and a man named Bossmiller were instrumental in perpetrating a fraud by collecting on cattle that were non-existent, and were not shipped to market. It is also clear that you made the entries in the books that allowed this fraud to happen. We're here to give you the chance to explain how and why you participated in this fraud, and to what extent you benefited."

Angela immediately began crying with her face into her hands. However, Julie noticed that in spite of her wailing, very few tears were produced. Julie took her turn at speaking. "Angela, we understand this is uncomfortable for you, but your participation clearly enabled this fraud. It's too late to turn back now. You must explain how you became involved."

Angela began her tale. "My brother Vincent and I never got along. He always bullied me and coerced me into doing things. After my husband died, there was no one to protect me from him. He would at times move into my apartment for several days and take money from me. If I didn't help him or objected, he would beat me. He and Sam got into gambling. They were making money, but not enough to keep up with their drinking and expensive life style."

"Who's Sam?"

"Sam Bossmiller. One day they came to me with their plan to become cattle brokers. But they didn't have any cattle. All they knew about cattle was what they learned from riding the trains and cheating the real cattle brokers. They bought just a few cattle and shipped them east. But they forced me to alter the books to show they shipped five more than the actual count. It worked and they collected. After that they made me do it several times. They would buy just a few to get passage on the train, but would inflate the numbers to collect more.

Toby asked, "Vincent and Bossmiller are on the books, but there is a third person. Who is Carter?"

Angela said, "I kept saying I couldn't do it anymore, so they said they would give me a share of their profit. But they didn't share anything. They made me add another name and I was supposed to collect under the name of Carter. But Vincent took that money too. I never got a thing out of it except a beating when I objected."

Toby asked, "Who else did Vincent and Bossmiller work with?"

"I don't know anybody else, except my son. They take him with them at times and disappear for several days. Kid likes them because they give him booze and make him feel like a big shot."

Julie interrupted, "Did you say kid? How old is he?"

"Max is my son. For some reason my brother, Fred, always calls him Kid. He is only sixteen, so I guess that's why."

Julie looked at Toby with an expression that spoke paragraphs. Toby slid his chair away from the two ladies, and Julie scooted hers closer to Angela.

"Angela, we have some dreadful news about your brother and your son."

"Oh no! What now?"

"Vincent, your son, and two others performed a train robbery a few days ago. They stole gold from the train and kidnapped two people from the train to hold as ransom."

Angela stared at Julie, apparently unmoved. "I always knew Vincent was up to bad things, and I knew it was bad for Kid to go with him. But there was nothing I could do. Where are they now?"

Julie, sensing Angela was not being entirely truthful, pulled the shock cord.

"I was one of the persons kidnapped. I was being held in their camp when I witnessed a disagreement. Your son asked for his share of the robbery loot. Vincent and Bossmiller, who appears to be the ring leader, declined to give your son anything. Instead they led him to the river and shot him. I believe they dumped his body into the flooding Yellowstone River."

This time Angela shed real tears. She bawled, "I should have run away. We should have hidden from him years ago."

Angela stopped her crying when she realized that there must be more to the story if Julie was before her in person, free from the kidnappers. "Then where is my brother Fred now?"

"I shot him twice. He's buried under a rockslide about six hundred miles from here", Julie said, trying to remove the ice from her tone. It was clear her soul was healing without remorse.

Toby continued to sit in silence, amazed at Julie's effective attack.

Angela no longer acted out her grief, but revealed her surprise at Julie's straightforwardness. It left Julie with an intimidating advantage.

Julie followed up with, "So now Angela, you are alone, with both your deeds and theirs. If you wish to clear yourself, and I think you should, you need to explain how your brother and Mr. Bossmiller learned when and where there would be a gold shipment, while the entire event was supposed to be kept secret."

There was silence. Toby said, "We are prepared to report this entire matter to the territorial Marshals, and that will include your participation. Your cooperation could also be mentioned."

Angela turned on the fake tears again and claimed to have nothing to do with the train robbery. She said, "Fred was in my office a couple of times. Maybe he looked over onto Vera's desk and saw her shipment books. I didn't even know there was going to be that kind of a shipment. She insisted her innocence by repeating the phrase several times.

Toby rose and left the room.

It was only a few strides to the office where Angela and Vera did their bookkeeping. Toby entered and wasted no time in explaining to Vera, his purpose. He was surprised to learn that Vera was expecting someone from the company to question her. She had learned of the train robbery not long after it happened. She said most of the office knew about it, including Angela.

Toby asked, "How well known was it, that there was going to be a shipment of gold picked up in Butte, Montana Territory?"

"Sir, it was to be a complete secret. I was not to tell anyone, and I didn't."

Toby pushed the point, "Was it possible that someone could have looked at your files when you were working on them, perhaps on your desk?"

"Absolutely not. Besides that, there was never anyone who ever came in here. This is just a bookkeeping room. We don't get many visitors in here."

"How about Angela?"

"This is a very small room. She sees much of what I do. But with things like this, I don't talk to her about it."

"Where do you keep the books when you aren't working on them?"

"We lock them up in that safe over there."

"We? Who's we?"

"Well, Angela and me."

"So you and Angela share the same safe?"

"Of course, it's the only one we have."

"Are you both always in this office together?"

"Most of the time, but we don't both stay here for lunch. We go at separate times so that there is always someone present. I usually bring my own lunch down to the lunch break room and eat with one of the other girls."

Toby leaned back in his chair and smiled. In a friendly tone he asked, "Vera, how long have you worked for the NP?"

She said, "Even before they laid the first track. I love it here, and the people are so nice. I sure wouldn't want something like this to change anything."

Toby thanked her and left.

The activity in the interview room was near an end when Toby returned. Angela denied she knew anything about the train robbery and could furnish nothing more about Bossmiller. The only real information she provided was Bossmiller's first name, "Sam", and the admission the name Carter was fictitiously used by her to share in the stock shipment fraud.

Toby signaled to Julie that they should terminate the interview. They needed to compare notes.

After conferring with NP officials, management agreed that Angela would be terminated. They chose not to seek prosecution at the time, but held on to the possibility depending on the results of the train robbery investigation.

Toby and Julie spent the rest of the day, discussing their options. They were not satisfied with Angela's statements, especially after Vera, an older reliable employee, furnished a direct contradiction. If they were to locate Bossmiller, they would have to learn more about him. They suspected Angela could contribute more. They decided to try one more time tomorrow.

* * * * *

The searching couple were in the superintendent's office only a moment after he arrived. They wanted one more session with Angela before dismissing her. An hour passed. Angela did not report for work. After two hours of waiting, they thanked the superintendent for his cooperation and mentioned they were going to Angela's apartment. Julie offered that perhaps Angela was grieving for her deceased son, although she doubted it.

Toby led Julie the few blocks to the shabby apartment complex. Inside the entry they viewed the mail box labels. Angela lived on the second floor. Bossmiller's name was still on the mailbox, but as before, the apartment number was not displayed on the box. It appeared his room was also on the second floor. Toby looked inside the box. It was empty.

Julie led, quietly climbing the stairs two steps at a time. Toby followed, treading on his toes. The creaking stair case betrayed their stealth, but no sounds could be heard from any of the rooms. Toby knocked on Angela's door. There was no answer, causing him to knock harder the second time. As he struck the door, the latch clicked and the door opened only the width of a hand. Toby pushed on the door and it swung open allowing unobstructed passage. Julie voiced a "Hello." There was no response. Again the greeting, but no response.

Both were already in the room, a combination kitchen and half parlor. Toby glanced, and repeated with a second look at an ash tray. It contained half of an extinguished cigar. At the end of a small davenport, a boot puller rested on its side. A pair of dirty men's socks drooped over the edge of a straw laundry basket.

Julie stepped further into the room and peered through the only other doorway. It led to the bedroom where she saw a sleeping Angela, in night clothes, with a pillow over her head. She called out, "Angela?" No response. "Angela, are you alright?" No response. She moved closer to the bed, and saw the bedding was twisted, ruffled, and partly wrapped around Angela's legs. Julie reached over, removed the pillow from her head and gasped. "Oh my God! She's dead!" The pillow, the blue toned skin and distended tongue lay bare the crime. Angela had been smothered.

Their first urge was to rush from the scene. Toby, not prone to panic said, "Wait Julie! We're already here, we must look now because we'll never get another chance. You can see a man was here quite recently. Don't touch anything, just observe."

As he spoke, he jarred a partially open armoire. In addition to Angela's clothes, hanging inside were two very large men's shirts, a similar sized vest and a man's belt.

Toby exclaimed, "Julie, Bossmiller has been living here. This has to be his clothing, and he is the only one I know that smokes those expensive cigars. I've seen him smoke a dozen of them playing poker."

Julie breathed, "Then he killed her. But why?"

Toby said, "Perhaps the answer lies with this." His foot rested on an object partially extending from under the bed. He pulled out into view a small canvass bag, open at the top, empty except for a few gold flakes.

Thirty-Three

The authorities in Spokane were efficient. They took statements from both Julie and Toby, checked their employment and confirmed that they were indeed the couple whom the NP reported as being abducted. The duo was reserved in providing valuable leads to find Bossmiller. Reality was, they were without anything specific, other than knowing he was only a few blocks from them the night before.

Toby made them aware of the obvious, directing them to the mailbox bearing Bossmiller's name. Two of the officers entered the apartment, only to find it almost totally bare. The only furnishings were those provided by the building management. An uncovered bed, two chairs and an empty closet were all they saw. It appeared the occupant left, taking any and all things that might identify him. The lawmen thought it ironic that he forgot to remove his name from the mail box. Just before leaving, Toby noticed a small trash bucket under the wash basin. From it he discreetly retrieved two pieces of crumpled paper, and secreted them in his pocket.

From the information he provided, Toby was able to convince the Marshal's the culprit was Bossmiller. He was confident they would confine their search to the Spokane area. However, Toby understood that the big man was a traveler. He would not linger in Spokane, but flee to other familiar territory, most likely to points east.

The NP twosome prepared messages to be distributed to all NP stations and train conductors from Spokane to St. Paul. The message was an alert to watch for Sam Bossmiller, provided his description and warned he was wanted for train robbery and suspected of murder. Sightings were to be reported immediately. Toby believed the bulk of the gold would still be stashed in the general vicinity of the robbery, and advised his superiors he was returning to Miles City.

******

Eddy began his search at the Pompey's river crossing. He retraced the route he and Jim had followed to where the freight wagon had been abandoned. To his surprise, he found the wagon was gone. He followed the now fading tracks back toward the railroad to where they joined the trail frequently traveled by the stagecoach. It was hopeless to try to trace them further. He returned to the river to track beyond the slough where the trail was lost several days before.

He searched all afternoon in the hot sun without finding a reasonable clue. The water in the slough had receded, revealing a well- traveled trail beyond, to the east. He followed hoof marks until they were joined by another faint set of wagon tracks.

He continued along the route for several miles until the valley widened. The river continued clinging to the sandstone cliffs on the north, but the trail curved back up toward the railroad and the stage route.

Eddy puzzled over the direction change. He thought, "If Bossmiller was transporting stolen gold, he would not travel on a populated route, especially not just after a well-publicized train robbery."

Once again, he turned toward the river. He continued along its banks, working his way through the cottonwoods and willows. In a particularly dense clump of brush he stopped to look at a beaver dam projecting across a narrow branch of the river. In the willows, partly covered by a fallen tree was a row boat. The vegetation around the boat indicated it had not been moved for several days.

The discovery sent warning signals all through his body. This part of the landscape would provide cover for a small army. He was vulnerable from all sides. He dismounted and tied his animals in the thicket. With his rifle in hand, he crept another one hundred paces down river. The brush abruptly terminated in a clearing. Barely above the flood line, a small homestead shack sat, surrounded by tall grass and weeds. Part of the roof had fallen over a makeshift porch. Windows were boarded up, but with cracks wide enough to see out from within. To the east side of the shack, a lean-to shed was large enough to shelter two horses. Curiously, the grass around the shed looked like it had been trampled or grazed. Between the shack and the shed was a stone-rimmed open well that also appeared to be beyond usable. On the west side of the primitive building was a weed covered dirt mound. From his position, he could not see an opening into the mound, but guessed it was a root cellar.

Eddy was sure this abandoned ruin might well serve as a temporary hiding place for both robbers and loot. But he dared not explore it alone because of all the perimeter brush and trees. He sat on the edge of the clearing and watched the building for over an hour. Satisfied it was vacant, he returned to his horse and pack mule.

He worked his way around the clearing and continued downriver to the east. Not another sign of human life appeared for three miles. He was about to return back upriver when he came upon an old trapper, living in an open shelter. Judging by the full firepit and accumulated litter, it appeared the old timer had been there for several weeks. Eddy asked the old man about the abandoned settlement upriver.

"Hey pardner, how ya doin'? How's the trapping along here?"

"Tain't good enough to share with anybody!"

"Oh, don't worry about me poaching your territory. I was just passing through. I figured I might stop in at the trading post a few miles downriver. I think they call it Custer."

"That's a couple days ride. It ain't much of a place though. He don't get much trading cause of the Sioux."

Eddy found the opening he needed to discreetly ask about the abandoned shack up river.

"How come you are camping here? Doesn't look like anyone's using the old place up river."

"Indians run the folks out of that place years ago. Nobody owns it now, but seems like the place is jinxed. Another feller lived there for a few months, but died. Once in a while a drifter holes up there, but not for long. I don't want nothing to do with the place. Seems to be a killin' ground for the Sioux."

"Anybody been there lately?"

"I seen a couple horses there 'bout ten days ago. Didn't stay long. They probably figgered out the place was haunted."

Eddy tried once more, "Makes you wonder what kind of drifters would take a chance on a place like that. What did they look like?"

"It weren't none of my business; a big feller. I stayed away from him."

That was good enough for Eddy. He circled back, gave the place another good look and decided he would come back another day with Toby.

Thirty-Four

They all met at Alice's home in Miles City. After a lengthy discussion, all the pieces fit together. Bossmiller, the undisputed leader of the crime wave against the NP, was on the run and probably in Montana Territory. Angela, Scar-neck,s sister, was fully involved in both the cattle shipment fraud, and the train robbery. She provided the information to set up both events. She even involved her own son, whom her brother and Bossmiller killed. The three questions remaining were; why did Bossmiller kill Angela, where did he hide the bullion, and where was he now? Eddy believed the bullion was located somewhere near the abandoned homestead east of the Pompey's river crossing near the banks of the Yellowstone. It would take time to explore the site, and for their safety they needed to post a guard while they searched. They could not afford to be surprised by Bossmiller, or any remaining friend. They even considered hiding in the heavily wooded perimeter and waiting, with the belief the big thief would return to the area. But it was not certain the gold was buried at the river site. The decision was made. They had to search the area themselves.

Involving another person would mean diluting the reward money. They truly missed Jim, but at the insistence of Julie, the plan included her, wherein Toby and Julie would search the old homestead while Eddy guarded the perimeter.

Again they left by freight train from Miles City, this time with three horses and the pack mule. The train discharged them at trackside, east of the Pompey's river crossing.

Just revisiting the area where she struggled so near death, made Julie uneasy. Eddy quickly led them downstream east of the train robber's camp. He slowed their progress as they approached the site of the hidden boat. After dismounting and inspecting the boat, Julie was certain it was the same boat she and Toby were transported in after the robbery. From there, they approached the old homestead on foot. Eddy led them in a circle around the dilapidated ruins, pointing out the old house, shed, cellar and well. Every item would have to be examined, and any earth showing recent disturbance had to be excavated.

Julie, armed with a shovel, and Toby armed with both a shovel and a rifle proceeded to the animal shed. Eddy entered the perimeter of trees after demonstrating a warning whistle he would sound if anyone was approaching. He admonished them to work quietly so that he could hear if anything was moving in the brush.

An examination of the shed produced nothing, although it appeared horses had been tied there not more than a week ago.

The old house was next. Rotting cottonwood logs formed its walls that boxed in only one room and a side porch. Part of the sod roof had caved in, and birds were nesting in the ridge beams. Rough sawn boards had been nailed over the windows. The door hung at a crippled slant by one hinge. Evidence of recent human trespass existed only on the damp earth floor. In addition to boot prints, dry grass had been spread to support a bed roll. The entire floor and walls were closely checked, resulting in no valuable discoveries.

Julie and Toby were exiting the old home when Eddy sounded his warning whistle. He gave two warnings, causing them to scramble in his direction. Crouched in the weeds, they waited to follow Eddy's instructions.

They watched as an old man, leading a sway-backed horse, emerged into the clearing. He slowly shuffled to the root cellar. They all lay quietly as the withered figure removed a shovel from his horse, and probed the slab of wood covering the entrance to the cellar. He slid the door aside and stepped down into the opening. The old trapper's back was turned to his observers. Eddy walked up behind the apparently nearly deaf man. With his rifle pointed toward the old codger, Eddy startled him with, "What are you doing?" Being too old to jump from fright, he began shaking from head to moccasins.

"Don't shoot me son, I'm gest explorin'."

"Exploring for what?"

The little man faced Eddy and whined, "Maybe I was a lookin' fer what you was a lookin to find."

"Take notice of this rifle mister, because you are jaw flapping me at the end of my worn-out hair trigger. Gimme' straight talk. Now why are you digging here?"

The old gent was shaking so badly he leaned over and sat on the edge of the decayed door. Eddy lowered the gun barrel and softened his approach. "You didn't level with me the other day."

"Well, I pretty much did. But I didn't give you all of it."

"Old partner, I think now might be a good time to hand over the rest of it."

"I told ya that a big feller was here for a day, and maybe a night. I was up there by the beaver dam and he come over real close but didn't see me. He stands a-lookin in the willows and twas then I sees a boat. He checks out the boat but didn't go no-wheres in it. Then he walks back to the house and commenced to diggin'. He didn't dig much more'n a few shovels and stopped. Then he goes down into the cellar. I couldn't see him no more, so I used my chance to git back around to the other side of the place.

The old fella continued, "Jist a lookin' at that guy gimme the spine shivers so I ain't been up here since. But when you come along and got to pesterin' me about the place, I figgered maybe you was a Marshal a-hidin' yer badge fer some reason; like maybe the guy was burying somethin' he shouldn't.

Sos I been a-watchin' the place, and there ain't nobody come back. I didn't see no harm in seein' what he was a-diggin' about. I was scared of that guy and didn't want to git in the corral all alone with a mean bull. So I jist thought I'd let you figger it out by yerself."

Eddy motioned for Toby and Julie to come out of hiding and offered a short explanation. "I and my friends over there are not Marshals. But we are working for the NP railroad. There was a train robbery, and we have reason to believe the big guy is in possession of a few things they took. We have been searching up and down the river for a few days, and will probably continue for a few more. I will tell you straight out that if the big guy learns you were watching him, or know anything about him, he will surely enjoy turning you into coyote meat. Or you could end up floating face down in the river, like the guy he cut out of his gang. So if you see him around here again, you better not tell him about us, and you better play dumb about everything."

"Yup, I've done that fer years. I won't say nuthin'."

Eddy concluded his lecture with, "Are you sure you have told me everything? Have you found or taken anything from here that the big guy left?"

"No sir-ee. I told you I was scared of him."

"OK then pardner. If you'll excuse us, we have some work to do. Maybe I'll drop in again in a few days to see how you are doing, and check to see if the big guy ever comes back. Now remember, keep your mouth shut and live through this."

The old trapper picked up his shovel, and rode off downriver, mumbling, "Gal-dangit, I thought it was jist the Indians that would be givin me troubles."

Eddy and Toby began digging in the soft dirt of the cellar floor. There wasn't room for three in the small space. Julie thoughtfully took Eddy's rifle and began watching for intruders. No more than a foot beneath the surface, the shovels struck wood. The lid of the placer gold shipping crate was still loosely attached to the original container. Toby pulled off the lid and looked down at five canvas sacks of gold dust and nuggets; only half of the original shipment.

After a long slow whistle, Eddy spoke first. "That makes sense. Bossmiller had to bury the shipment here because he couldn't carry it all. Five sacks are about all he could travel with, and one of them turned up empty under that gal's bed in Spokane. I'm still betting that the bullion, those gold bars, are around here someplace too."

Toby said, "Well at least we got some of it. This is enough to prove the case, but not enough to recover the reward. Let's put this stuff onto the mule, and keep looking."

They returned to the cellar, and reburied the empty crate, smoothing the earth to look like it had not been disturbed. Although they probed the rest of the cellar floor, they found it to be solid, not concealing anything additional.

The excitement of the discovery caused them to relax their sentinel vigil. All three searched the ground within the clearing. The tall river grass appeared undisturbed. As Julie walked near the well, she noticed a few of the weeds were visibly bent. She looked into the open, hand dug, well, and exclaimed, "Ugh, that water certainly doesn't look drinkable. There's bugs and grass and all sorts of stuff down there."

An old rope was tied to a weathered timber braced across the perimeter stones. The other end of the rope hung loosely down into the water, and was apparently tied to a wooden bucket. The darkness at the water line prevented her from seeing the condition of the old relic and, out of curiosity, she pulled on the rope to lift the bucket. As soon as the bucket was above the water, she exclaimed, "Good heavens, that's heavy."

The more she pulled to raise the bucket, the heaver it got until she was struggling to lift if further. She called out, "Hey guys. Come over here and look at this."

Both of the men came to her aid and began to raise the water bucket. They could not see the cause of the extra weight until the container reached the top. Attached to its bottom was a cable. They pulled on the cable until a third object emerged. A set of pulleys, configured into a block and tackle, was rigged to something still submerged in the well. A glance around the weeds near the well disclosed an out of place cottonwood log, freshly cut just the right length to span over the stone perimeter. With the log in place, and the pulley system secured to it, they hoisted up a large wooden crate. Joyous, with great excitement, they pried loose the top to see multiple grimy, muddy, gold bars. It took all three of them to get the crate over the well rim and onto the ground.

They viewed the container, wide eyed and jubilant. Toby stood at the edge of the well, wiping the slime from one of the exposed bars, about to question if any were missing, when a horse whinnied. It came from outside the clearing to the south. It was not from one of their horses. No one was yet in sight. Julie ran in the direction of their horses by the river, while Toby and Eddy jumped into the nearest brush on the east side of the clearing's edge. But there was a problem. Eddy's rifle was fifteen paces away, leaning on the cattle shed. Toby's gun was at the side of the house, the direction in which Julie ran. As she rounded the corner of the building, Toby saw her grab the gun and disappear into the trees, hopefully to keep their own horses from answering the call.

Hushed in the weeds, they saw a big man on an oversized chestnut horse. Bossmiller road into view. Unaware that he was not alone, he rode across the clearing in the direction of Julie. As he reached the side of the clear cut nearest the river, he dismounted, very near to where Julie lay silent in the tall grass. Off his horse, he stretched and looked around the clearing. The wooden crate was on the far side of the well, out of his view, but the log across the top rested proudly above the weeds. The big man did not step back to remove his rifle from the scabbard, but set his attention on the well. As he strode toward the well, Julie sprang from her retreat to quickly snatch the rifle from Bossmiller's saddle. She disappeared back into the grass unseen by the enemy. When he reached the well, he saw the open crate on the far side. It was as if he woke from a trance. He whirled around in time to see Eddy sprint toward his rifle resting against the shed. Bossmiller drew a revolver from his hip and pulled the trigger. He fired before he took aim, and the projectile cut through the grass, landing behind Eddy. He pulled the trigger again and only a brittle "click" was heard. Two more pulls resulted only in shallow clicks as Eddy dove around the shed, rifle in hand.

When Eddy realized the big man's hand gun was malfunctioning, he appeared with the rifle pointed at the big target. Bossmiller moved as if to attempt another shot, when Eddy fired his rifle, purposefully missing to the side.

Eddy shouted, "Drop the gun, or the next one's going into your gut." Bossmiller hesitated and Eddy hollered, "I'm not wasting any more shells on you. That's your only warning. Now drop it."

As Bossmiller turned loose of the revolver, he saw Toby rise out of the grass to his left. In a desperate effort, big Sam turned and clumsily ran toward his horse. As he neared Julie, she rose out of the grass with her rifle aimed at the approaching hulk. She shouted, "Stop right there or I'll blast your legs off."

Eddy in pursuit shouted, "Don't kill him till he talks."

She hesitated, and in that brief moment, Bossmiller turned to his left and ran past Julie, in the direction of the boat. Both Eddy and Toby were much faster than the heavy runner. As Bossmiller reached the boat, Toby arrived in time to grab an arm. With a show of strength, Bossmiller grabbed an oar and swung it, connecting with Toby's ribs. Eddy, who had been running with his rifle arrived just in time for Toby to fall backwards causing them to both crash into the willows. Bossmiller shoved the boat out into the current and set the oars into the locks.

Julie, seeing the man beginning his escape, fired her rifle into the bow of the boat. Eddy, once again was shouting, "Don't kill him. Just sink the boat."

With both of them firing into the wooden hull, they ripped a large chunk out of the bow. The boat quickly began taking on water, and the weight of the big man was sinking it fast.

Bossmiller saw his plight and shouted, "I can't swim! I can't swim! Don't let me drown!"

Eddy quit firing, looked at Julie with raised eyebrows and said, "Oh crap! I never thought of that."

Toby realized the problem and was running down river, still keeping up with the sinking boat. He shouted, "Get out to that little sandbar."

Bossmiller looked to his left and thrust with all his strength to get the boat turned toward a thin sandbar ten yards from the bank. As the sinking boat rolled to its side, the submerged bow caught the gravel edge of the little island and flipped, throwing its contents into the water. Bossmiller landed at the shallow edge of the sand bar and crawled out of the water. The boat split apart and drifted downriver. Bossmiller, looking like a soaked hippopotamus, sat in the sand panting. When he could breathe again, he shouted, "You damn fools nearly killed me."

"Well, we ain't done yet", was Eddy's reply.

Only thirty feet of deep rushing water separated their fugitive from them. If he was truthful about not being able to swim, Bossmiller was trapped.

Eddy began laughing. "Now ain't you a pretty sight, out there all by yourself. I don't suppose the mosquitos could suck you dry overnight, could they? I guess we'll know by morning."

The pathetic hulk screamed, "You can't leave me out here. I told you I can't swim. If the water rises over night, I'll drown."

Eddy said quietly to his friends, "Woops, that's right. He's worth too much money to let drift down the river. Let's go get the rope out of the mule pack. But first let's pretend to walk away."

They all enjoyed hearing him plead as they retreated out of sight. But then Eddy said, "You guys go get the rope. I'm going to watch, just to make sure he's not lying. If he jumps in and swims down river, I'd be tempted to shoot him."

Eddy watched as the big man tiptoed to the water's edge. He backed away, and looked up and down the river. He paced all the way around the little island sand bar, checking the depth of the water. Frustrated, he stood hatless in the middle of the island and gazed in the direction the three had gone. Eddy was convinced Bossmiller could not swim. He was also thinking that a rescue was going to be a problem.

Toby returned with a lariat Eddy had the foresight to pack. They were concerned that the bulk of the man could pull them both into the river because the current was strong between the island and the bank where they stood. Toby came up with a plan.

"Let's see what we can get out of him while he is still on the island. If he won't say anything or keeps lying, we'll get the rope around his chest with a pretend rescue. But we'll leave him suspended midstream until he is about to meet the devil or Jesus, and see what he says then."

They began by trying to throw the rope across the span of water. Neither Toby nor Eddy could toss the rope far enough for it to land on the sand bar because the willows on the bank prevented them from swinging the rope in a centrifugal loop. Finally Julie approached with a piece of wood she bound in the lariat loop, creating a throwing weight. Eddy began twirling the rope until it again hung up in the willow branches near the water's edge. Several more attempts and a lucky bounce landed the wood chunk near Bossmiller's feet. He looked back at his tormenters and said, "Now what am I supposed to do?"

Eddy had the most experience dealing with unsavory characters and Toby was happy to have him do the talking. Anytime Eddy produced a threat, he was convincing.

Eddy's reply was, "Well old buddy, we ain't going to do anything until you tell us a few things."

"Like what?"

"Like the rest of the gold."

"I spent it."

"No you didn't. You can't spend that much in a week."

"I lost it gambling."

"No you didn't. You weren't riding the rails or hanging out at any of your gambling joints. Now if you're gonna waste our time, standing out there lying, I'm gonna leave your ass on that sandbar until the winter ice pushes you downriver. Now where did you hide the gold dust?"

"I gave it to Angela."

"All of it?"

"Yah."

"And she's still got it?

"Yah."

"And what about the bullion bars, where are they?"

"Well you got most of them."

"Most of them?" The answer was a surprise. None of the group knew that any of the bars were missing because the crate was nearly full.

"Yah, I gave a couple of them to Angela too."

Eddy turned to Toby and softly said, "I think he's ready for the rope, mid-stream style."

Toby instructed Bossmiller to put the loop of the lariat around his chest, just below his armpits, with the long loose end extending out in front of him. Big Sam complied. Toby pulled the line taunt and handed the middle of it to Eddy. He backed away with the remaining length and looped one turn around a cottonwood branch that extended several feet out over the river. He brought the far loose end back to the shoreline where he stopped next to Eddy.

Bossmiller asked, "What's the loop over the tree for?"

Toby said, "That's just in case we can't hold you. We don't want you drifting down the river with our good rope."

The big guy was scared or he would have seen through Toby's ruse. If Toby was correct, when Eddy let go of the line, it would snap straight from the branch over the water. The current would hold Bossmiller out in the middle of the stream until the loop was removed from the tree. He and Eddy still had control of the far end so Bossmiller could eventually be towed to the river's edge.

Julie, without being told, could see what was going to happen. It was difficult for her to stifle a snicker. She just hoped her partners could pull the big tub to shore after he was half drowned.

With everything set, Eddy called out, "OK, we gotcha. Step off into the water."

The big, supposedly brave, man was really a coward when it came to water. He stepped to the edge of the sand bar and looked at the passing torrent. He stepped back and stared at Eddy saying, "You sure about this?"

Eddy, enjoying himself said, "Ah, come on you big baby. Hang on to the rope and step on in."

Bossmiller put one foot in the sandy edge, raised the other and fell sideways into the stream causing a big splash. As soon as he was on his belly a couple feet from the sand bar, Eddy turned loose of his rope. The couple seconds of slack rope caused Bossmiller to dip under the water until the rope was taunt again, between him and the overhanging tree branch. It took only seconds more until he was bobbing like a porpoise, holding onto the rope while it drew ever tighter around his puffy chest. It took considerable effort for him to hold his head above the rush of water splashing over his shoulders.

"Pull me in, or I'm gonna sink."

Eddy jeered, "Sink, no, drown, maybe."

"Your lying, you *(too profane to print.)*"

"You wanna stay out there cussing, or do you want to tell me where the rest of the gold is?"

Bossmiller was coughing water, unable to keep his face above the steady pressure. "It's in Spokane."

"Where?"

His voice was beginning to come in gargled spurts. "I put it right under your nose. It's in a rental locker in the Spokane train depot."

"All of it?"

"Yes, three bars and four bags."

"Why did you kill Angela?"

"I didn't kill nobody. Now get me out of here. I can't hold on much longer."

"You're drowning is going to be sort of like Angela smothering. It won't hurt, you're just gonna run out of air."

Bossmiller said nothing for a few seconds until his hand slipped and his entire head went under. Julie looked at Eddy as if to ask whether he was really going to let the man drown.

When he bobbed to the surface he bellowed, "She got greedy. When you guys told her that her brother was dead, she decided she should have all of his share. Fred planned to leave her without anything anyway. I told her no, and she said she was going to turn me in if I didn't give her half of everything. So I did her in the easy way."

Eddy said nothing and looked at Toby, who asked one more question, "What's the locker number?"

"I don't know, I can't remember."

"Ok pardner, let's see how much more water you can swallow before you sink."

"No, No please. It's the bottom one on the right side of the longest row. That's it, but I just can't remember the number."

Toby nodded at Eddy and slid out onto the limb holding the rope. He jerked the loop to the side, freeing it from the tree. The line went slack, sending Bossmiller deep into the current. Eddy stood on the bank with the end of the rope firmly in his hand. But when the big man drifted to the end of the slack, the rope jerked Eddy like a steer in a rodeo. His feet slid on the soft river bank until Julie grabbed both him and the rope. The two held on until Toby was able to come to their side.

By the time they pulled out their catch, he was in no condition to resist. They drug him up the bank and let him cough until his lungs expelled most of the water. Toby searched him for weapons and found nothing. The discarded revolver now lost in the tall grass was all he carried.

Eddy said, "What? No gun? Heck, I need to find the one he dropped in the grass, and look at why it quit working. I'm still alive mostly because Mr. B is a bad shot." He grinned and looked at Julie saying, "I'd rather be lucky than good. By the way, thanks for helping out. I don't swim so good with my boots on either."

Thirty-Five

Their next problem became one of transportation. They had more weight than their horses and mule could carry. Bossmiller could be tied to his own horse, but the gold was heavy. They didn't dare to leave it, even if it was reburied.

Eddy said, "Sometimes when I have a problem, I think of Jim and come up with the answer. Let's make an Indian type of drag. If we go slow, we can make it up to Clermont."

Toby said, "Good, there's a little depot there and we can all board a train to Miles City. I don't want to struggle all the way to Billings. There's a Judge and Marshal in Miles City. But we'll have to find an open cattle car for the horses."

Bossmiller was tied to his horse, hands to the saddle horn and legs bound together by a rope running under the saddle cinch. For additional security, Eddy looped a rope around the big man's neck and held it in his hands. The gold drug behind the mule who balked at the contraption every few minutes.

They located the stage road, and traveled only a half mile when the westbound coach rolled into view. Toby flagged down the driver, while the "shotgun rider" aimed at Eddy. A quick explanation got their cooperation and the heavy baggage was loaded aboard the stage. Eddy sat on top guarding Bossmiller, leaving Toby and Julie to follow behind with the horses. They made good time and arrived at the little depot by late afternoon. Three empty cattle cars sat on a siding.

Toby greeted the depot agent and determined he was well acquainted with most circumstances of the train robbery. The agent was busy making arrangements to stop the next eastbound train, when a small boy entered the office. Seeing that the man was busy, he ran back outside and confronted the bound prisoner.

"Hey mister. You still owe me fifty cents." Bossmiller only grunted at the boy who ran back into the depot and shouted, "Hey grandpa! That man who gave me the note is tied on a horse outside."

Toby took fifty cents from his pocket and gave it to the boy. "What's your name son?"

"My name's Little Al, cause my Dad's Big Al, and my Grandpa's Old Al."

Toby knew he just added one more element to a conviction, and a fine reward.

The eastbound freight hooked onto one of the empty cattle cars. Eddy loaded the animals while Toby and Julie got into the caboose with their cargo. Eddy put Bossmiller on the floor of the dirty cattle car, bound hand and foot. Eddy rode inside the car with his back against the headwall and the rifle on his lap. His prisoner whined about lying in the filth for three of the five-hour journey.

Old Al made arrangements for the cattle car prison to be met by two U.S. Marshals. They escorted the manure-soaked Sam Bossmiller to the Territorial Jail. They also took possession of the valuable cargo.

Julie, Eddy and Toby spent most of the following day making statements to the local lawmen. Toby gave them the small crumpled paper he retrieved from the waste can in Angela's room. It contained numbers, in two groupings. Toby suggested it may be the number of a storage locker in the Spokane Railroad Depot, or even the combination to a simple lock.

Eddy returned to find a bank draft of ten thousand dollars, rewarding him for the rescue of Toby and Julie. The Miles City Depot agent ceremoniously presented him with the money along with written commendations from NP management.

Together, the trio applied for the additional rewards totaling thirty thousand for capturing Bossmiller and recovering the stolen cargo. Superintendent Hanson promised the money would be delivered after a review of the legal reports.

The three victors agreed to split the money three ways, giving Eddy another ten, while twenty would go to Julie and Toby.

* * * * *

An in-court hearing was conducted concerning the multiple deaths resulting from the train robbery and kidnapping. It was resolved from victim testimony and confessions of Bossmiller that all deaths, were the result of criminal activities perpetrated by the deceased, and from the efforts of the victims defending themselves. Eddy explained that after the shooting of Jim Little Bear, by Bolo, he in return shot Bolo in self-defense. The judge made Eddy describe where, why, and how he buried Jim. Eddy struggled with his emotions during the explanation. The judge became quite sympathetic and excepted his narration, after which he did not question him about the burial of Bolo, or Vincent. The death of Sanchez, scalped and hanging from a tree was known only by Bossmiller and was never mentioned or addressed.

Julie boldly testified before the judge, saying she morally objected to killing a human but given the circumstances, which she described, she would do it again to save her and another's life. She said, "I stand before you today with great regret that I was forced to fire that rifle at Vincent, but with no remorse that I did so."

The judge solemnly stated, "Madam, I am honored to have in the presence of this court, a woman who has suffered with such strength, who is so brave as to confront the vilest of criminals, and who as you have demonstrated, has the will to not be intimidated or remorseful. The court hereby absolves you and your associates of all responsibilities concerning the deaths in this matter. May you all live on in strength and innocence."

He concluded with, "The disposition of Mr. Bossmiller will be continued in a separate proceeding. Court Dismissed."

* * * * *

At the end of the long administrative day, Eddy gathered them all together at Alice's home. He announced that a wedding was planned in the near future. He asked Toby and Julie if they would be able to remain in Miles City for two more days. They were not anxious to return to the big city and Julie was thrilled to be asked to participate in the ceremony.

Thirty-Six

A little chapel, first used as a meeting place by Toby and Julie five years prior, was the perfect place for the small gathering. Toby was the best man, Julie the matron of honor. Timmy brought in a gold ring. Coworkers of Eddy, and Alice attended the brief ceremony. Alice Horton, a beautiful bride with shiny black hair curling over a white satin gown, became Mrs. Alice Kingston.

Timmy's friends, Chubby and Joe were in attendance. After the ceremony, Joe and Chubby gathered around Timmy while Chubby asked, "Did you ask him?

Timmy said, "No, not yet."

"Well, when you gonna ask him?"

"I have to wait until all the people leave."

"Well shoot, that may not be until tomorrow."

"We'll have time. We just have to wait, cause this is gonna be a personal thing."

Chubby concluded with, "OK, but remember we wanna be there too."

The evening was spent in conversation. Each couple shared their hopes for the future. While Julie and Toby expressed their uncertainty concerning the disposition of their historical homesteads, Eddy surprised them with his plans.

"I'm not cut out to be a railroad man. I'm better off working things my own way. Back when Jim and I were roaming around busting broncs, I made friends with a blacksmith. He made a lot of horseshoes. I helped him a couple of days, and really liked it. It wasn't just the shoes, but the whole operation. The guy made stuff out of scrap iron, forged things together, built windmills, and repaired stuff from all over the territory. He has a shop in Billings now, but he's getting old and wants to quit. If I worked with him for a few months, I could buy his shop and run it. He has more work than he can keep up with. With the extra money I have now, I know I could build that place up into a big operation. Alice is willing to move with me, and we'll start everything new together.

Toby and Julie, with jealous attention, gave them their full encouragement.

Thirty-Seven

The next day Julie and Toby departed on the morning passenger express. Once again, the train staff treated them like royalty, since now they were the heroic survivors of a robbery and kidnapping. Both longed to be ignored. Normalcy was now an elusive commodity. There were many serious adjustments to be made in the near future. Eddy's bold departure announcement provoked more independent thought.

The first day back for Toby was confusing. He received praise for his actions, but detected jealousy and resentment of the overall accomplishment. Some felt it was his duty to capture Sam Bossmiller and recover the gold, and that he should do it without a cash award. He even heard the word sensationalism used concerning the subject. However, his best allies, Mr. Hanson and the company lawyer, Mr. Lavine, stood by him.

Julie did not go to work. She was given a leave of absence several days prior by Mr. Hanson, and was in no hurry to return to the incompetence of Piddledinger. She was still dealing with the estate of her mother and aunt.

A serious letter awaited her attention. The bank managing her ranch advised the property was not being used to its capacity. According to the advisory letter, the rancher leasing the property was unable to finance additional cattle to fully utilize the rangeland. The suggestion was that Julie use any available funding she possessed to purchase more cattle, and allow them to be under the bank's supervision. They suggested the range could support an additional five-hundred head. Although it was a partial answer to her decision concerning what she should do with the land, she also had some serious doubts. She was happy to have Toby home soon to discuss it.

* * * * * *

Timmy wasted no time in telling Chubby and Joe about his possible move to Billings. Timmy was excited, but the other two decried the change. Two days after the wedding, they met Eddy at the corrals. The little gang wanted to know if they could continue counting livestock. Eddy explained that he was proud of the way they conducted themselves and accomplish their jobs, however, their services were no longer needed. He told them why.

There was a quiet pause, and Chubby turned to Timmy, and blurted, "Did you ask him?"

Timmy said, "No!"

Eddy, still with them questioned, "Ask me what?"

Chubby said, "We wanted you to teach us how to cuss."

Eddy broke out laughing. "Why in the world would you want to know that?"

Joe said, "Every guy needs to know how to cuss. You need it in times when everything goes bad. They don't teach us nothing like that in school. You know everything Eddy, and we hoped you might show us how to use some real good words."

Eddy stopped laughing when he realized the young men were serious. It was a compliment that they looked to him for so many things, but this request required a thoughtful answer.

Eddy said, "Boys, sometimes you have to learn things in a specific order. One of the smartest guys I know doesn't cuss. His mother taught him to learn every word possible that was not a cuss word, so that he could say very intelligent things without cussing. It made him a better all-around man. Now, I don't expect you guys to sit in a dark room and memorize a dictionary. And I'll admit that sometimes a person feels like he just needs a good cuss word. But first I think you need to learn to pray. If you learn how to pray, you won't need to know a lot of cuss words. But there are rules to praying."

Eddy sat them down around him and continued. "First of all, don't pray when it rains, if you don't pray when the sun shines." He looked at them and asked, "Do you know what that means?"

Joe nodded his head and replied, "Don't just pray when things are bad and you need something."

Eddy knew he now had their attention. "Yes, too many use prayers as a crutch, thinking they always need help instead of helping themselves. It's better to pray for someone else rather than always for yourself. You have to be strong on your own. Don't grow a wishbone where your backbone ought to be. Chubby, the reason you don't know how to cuss is that you aren't supposed to know how. Boys shouldn't be cussing. Just like you wouldn't paint your house a bad color to have it noticed, you don't want to paint yourself in a bad way, to be noticed. Yes, I know that sometimes you feel you just need to say something bad in terrible situations. In time, you will learn what might fit the occasion. But never let yourself get into the habit of using that kind of language just to make yourself sound tough or to get noticed. It will never help you look good. You will make yourself a much prouder person if you learn a thousand good words for every one cuss word. So, use good words in prayers, and speak like well-mannered educated young men."

When Eddy finished, one of the boys mumbled thank you, and they shuffled off together.

Chubby said, "Geez, I didn't expect that."

Joe said, "Maybe we should have asked him for a dictionary."

Timmy who was willing, if necessary, to take a beating defending Eddy, said, "Hey, you know he is right. I'm sure he was talking about his friend Toby. That guy can make you feel stupid with his words, and they're a lot stronger than cuss words. He didn't say we could never cuss. He just meant we should study good words and only store up a few of the others when we came across them."

Joe said, "Yah, I think I got that. But anyway, I'm glad we asked him. I don't think a guy could go wrong following Eddy's advice."

Chubby said, "Well, after all that, I guess praying for someone to teach me how to cuss is out of the question."

Then he changed the subject. "Timmy, if you move to Billings with Eddy, are you ever going to come back?"

Timmy replied with something he only hoped, "Sure, we'll never stop coming back to visit you guys."

Thirty-Eight

As soon as Toby arrived home, Julie presented him with the bank letter. As usual, he gave it some thought before he spoke.

"That's very interesting. What do you think?"

Julie had been thinking about it all afternoon. She shared her thoughts. "They want me to actually invest money with them, at least indirectly. I'm supposed to put up the money, and they manage it. If things go well, they keep a percentage and I get the rest. If things go bad, I lose the money, and they lose nothing."

"That's pretty much the picture. A long time ago, Eddy gave me a lecture. One of the important things he said was one should never let anyone else handle your money. I didn't have any at the time, but I have since realized it was very good advice. The proposal leaves you with two unknowns. Who will be the people managing the money, and who will be the rancher taking care of the cattle?"

Julie smiled, "I'm glad to hear you say that, because I have the same feeling. What troubles me most is this: Do you think we, you and I, could make it as cattle ranchers, or even farmers?"

"No, we couldn't. Not yet. But if we spend from now until spring at the library, if we read everything written about range management, cattle production, animal husbandry, and dry land farming, we probably could. You know old friends and neighbors up there. We could consult them along with what we learn studying. I'm not naïve enough to think you can learn all that stuff from books. But I do know that, whether you think you can, or whether you think you can't, you're right."

Julie laughed, "Well that's pretty clever. I like the idea of getting educated. OK, if you want to try it, I'll decline this bank offer, and we'll introduce ourselves to the library for the winter. It will give us more time to choose wisely."

Toby mused, "We now have a nice sum of money put away. We could afford to experiment with the profession for a year, before we make a large commitment. The ranch house is livable after a good cleaning, and there certainly is enough land between the two of us to get started."

Julie bubbled with excitement. "How far is the library? I can hardly wait to begin."

"It's about a half mile to the south. There's one more thing. Mr. Lavine spoke to me about this, but we have been so involved with other things, I have not mentioned it. He lectured me about the homestead act of 1862. President Lincoln signed it into law twenty-four years ago. That's how our parents got started; with free land granted to each person. Probably your parents increased their land by buying homesteads from others who went broke and sold cheap. Mr. Lavine said there are many old homesteads out there that are still for sale. "

Julie asked, "Was he suggesting that we buy land somewhere else?"

"Not really. It's more complicated than that. The government gave millions of acres of land to the railroads. He said about a hundred seventy-five million acres were given to the NP and a couple other railroads. The NP owns land ten miles wide, on both sides of the tracks, all across the country from St. Paul to the Pacific Ocean. They don't own everything in the ten-mile-wide swath because it is like a checker board. They own every other section."

"Wow!" Julie asked, "Why did they give them so much?"

They expected the railroads to sell the land to settlers, and use the money to build the tracks. But people didn't want to buy the land until they saw the actual rails and trains. It is only after the trains were moving through the territories, that towns are being built."

"Toby, so where are you going with all this. How does it affect us?"

"Mr. Lavine says, as railroad employees, we can purchase chunks of NP land at a big discount. If we buy in preferred places, we can then trade or resell the property in exchange for ranch land. We could probably work a few deals to expand our holdings in the Musselshell."

"That would be fantastic. But we would have to buy from the NP before we terminated our employment."

"That's right. But if you're interested, and I am, I can discuss it more with him. Confidentially he has already done a little trading, and is planning to do more. I'm sure he will offer his guidance. I personally think investing in more land is safer than buying cows that would be running around under somebody else's supervision. We can always sell the land later, and most likely at a profit. Apparently, Mr. Lavine is doing well with it."

Julie said, "I would certainly be happy with that. We could secure the land, venture into the ranch experiment, and then decide if we wanted to stay and grow. We surely should be able to decide after a year, and meanwhile, our money could be in land that was gaining in value. OK Toby, I think we are going to be good partners."

Both returned to their jobs, but were pre-occupied with their new outside interests. After two weeks passed, Toby returned home with exciting news. He told Julie, "I talked to Mr. Lavine today about purchasing NP land. He said they were anxious to sell, but more importantly they were concerned about paying our reward in cash. He attended a board meeting where he suggested the company pay us off with a land grant. He said the board members were in favor of it, and left it to him to arrange the deal if we would accept it. It would then cost them nothing, and we could benefit probably more from the land than we could the cash. It would be simple with no broker fees, no bank drafts and all that other stuff."

This time it was Julie's time to say, "What do you think?"

"Right now we don't need cash. You haven't even settled your Aunt's estate, but you already know there will be considerable cash available when you finish. I think this may be a tremendous opportunity. All we need to do is bargain as many acres as possible out of them. The mineral rights don't go with the land, but Mr. Lavine suggested we negotiate for timber and farm land. People like my old boss, Tom Teel, the chief surveyor, can point us toward the good locations. Mr. Lavine says, because we are part of the NP, we might be able to get good property for about seven dollars an acre, which is almost half the average price."

"I can't ever remember when half price wasn't a good deal" said Julie. Then she was silent for a few moments and adopted a sad tone when she said, "I know it's almost a fairy tale opportunity, but I can't erase from my mind, some of the terrible things that happened. I feel soiled benefiting from the human wreckage of greed. It is greed and lawlessness that vaulted us into prosperity. How shall I ever be proud of that?"

Toby didn't respond immediately, and finally chose his words carefully. "I have labored with some of the same thoughts. It becomes complicated, but the solution has moral acceptance. The first premise is that we did not ask for any of this trauma, or the rewards that followed. For heaven's sake we were on our honeymoon. Moreover, I was directed to look into the activities that grew into a major crime spree.

Together, and with the help of Eddy and poor Jim, we succeeded in extinguishing it, in part because the gang self-destructed. It is the social structure of our society, and the institutional custom of law enforcement to offer rewards to gain citizen participation. We happened to be in the right place at the right time to earn those rewards."

It was evident to Julie that Toby too, had given the matter much thought. He continued, "An additional point that challenges self-respect, is the question of how shall we deal with the gains. I believe the soil you feel from the benefits would become a visible brand of shame if we spent it lavishly and flaunted our gains beyond our social level. However our company, and our jobs have placed a ceiling above our heads that we cannot easily penetrate. Reality is, we are still looked upon as "kids" within the company and are thought of as servants to the business class. The guilt we feel comes from the empathy we have for our friends and associates who toil with us under that ceiling. We are definitely living in a class system. A perfect example is your boss, Piddledinger. He is in the business class, where his incompetence is ignored because of an accident of birth; he is the nephew of the president. For little other reason, he is accepted into his social club, wears an expensive bowler, and hovers above us without beating a wing. We should not feel guilt for breaking through the ceiling. Tell me who else has eaten rattle snake to stay alive. Who among us has endured midday heat and parched bleeding lips from rationing brackish water that was strained through a shirt? How many have huddled among rocks while being hunted by killers? Who else bares scars on his chest, cut by the hands of thieves? Remember the promise you made to yourself? I remember. You said that if we should live, you would grasp the end of the rainbow and live as vibrant as the colors within. We have been blessed with the opportunity to break through the class ceiling, and become business people, working for ourselves. We should feel no shame in being rewarded for our accomplishments."

At the end of his lecture, Julie said, "Toby, you are the only man without a pulpit that can set my soul at rest. You have washed me clean. I believe we can still live humbly at the end of the rainbow."

Toby said, "I'll start working on it tomorrow. Now, let's get down to the library."

Thirty-Nine

The fall season faded into winter. The holidays brought postal greeting from friends. Among the most cherished was a letter from Eddy and Alice. Eddy was enjoying his apprenticeship of blacksmithing and metal fabrication. Timmy was excelling in his new school, and Alice was working part time in a mercantile. They were living comfortably in a home, the result of trading her father's house in Miles City. Eddy expected to own the Billings business by early summer.

Toby and Julie catalogued their research into voluminous hand written copies, making an agricultural and ranching library of their own. Both were gaining confidence in their ability to successfully farm and ranch in Montana Territory.

Toby acquired four and a half sections of land from the NP at seven dollars per acre, in exchange for the reward earned from recovering a fortune in gold and apprehending Sam Bossmiller. The land, selected with the help of chief surveyor, Teel, was located in several regions of expected expansion and prosperity.

Julie was meticulously selecting from her Aunt's and Mother's estate, items to retain for shipment to her ranch in Montana Territory. The remainder she sorted out to be sold or given to her Aunt's church friends.

On January ninth, 1887, an act of nature again affected their lives. A blizzard, later known as the Blizzard of 1887, struck Montana Territory and the broad Northern plains. The storm dumped an average of sixteen inches of snow onto the rangeland, and followed with temperatures of fifty degrees below zero.

Ranchers were complacent due to several past winters of mild temperatures and ample range grass. They were content to leave their cattle to forage out in the open. But the winter of 1886-87 began with sparse grass due to a hot dry summer. Cattle left out on the range died by the thousands. Frozen and starved animals were stacked on the plains. Many floated away during the spring thaws. A count after the storm disclosed that at least ninety percent of all cattle in the Territories of Montana and the Dakotas died. It was now being called, "The great die up."

The news struck Toby and Julie like another death in the family. Their confidence in their future endeavor melted with the spring thaw. Letters from their bank managers bore only bad news. Many ranchers in the Musselshell area were bankrupt, including those working her property. Homesteads were for sale at extraordinarily low prices. Entire populations were migrating to the towns and cities.

Toby, always the learner and optimist again saw opportunities. He told Julie, "We haven't lost a thing. Land around your ranch will become available at prices lower than they have been for years. The lesson to be learned is that to avoid a similar disaster, we will need to diversify. We should expand into areas where we can farm the land in addition to just raising cattle. More of that tall grass that normally goes to waste during good years needs to be cut and stored as hay. We will of course need to accumulate farming equipment as well as hire farm hands. But our parents were not able to hire help because they never had the means to finance a start. We more than have a starting financial base. We can already trade sections of land along the railroad for extensively more in our former home area. We can expand to the extent our base will allow. We need to make our move as soon as spring breaks."

Together they made their decision. With hearts full of excitement for their new adventure west, back into Montana Territory, the couple began writing their letters of resignation to the Northern Pacific Railroad.

Acknowledgements

It takes a team to produce a written story. There are many who assisted in producing *Just Across the River.* Thanks go to Peggy Biekert, Connie Lien, and Sandra Phifer for editing, Neal Gunnels for marketing, Tiffani Anderson for river photo access, my wife Patty for research, and numerous friends for suggestions and tolerance during morning coffee.

Special thanks go to the people who now live in the land that has grown out of Montana Territory. The unmatched character of those living in Miles City, Roundup, Musselshell County, Billings, the Huntley Project and much of Montana, has provided the template for this adventure.

www.ingramcontent.com/pod-product-compliance
Lightning Source LLC
LaVergne TN
LVHW020538100826
845148LV00010B/1516

* 9 7 8 1 7 3 5 5 8 0 6 3 0 *